ADVENTURES ON PANT MOUNTAIN

On a dark night on the ridge of Panther Creek Mountain, Clay, 11, and Luke, 9, watched their room light up as lightning flashed through the window of their attic bedroom in their little cabin home. The driving rain hammered the tin roof with a sound that was deafening. It was magical. Clay and Luke snuggled beneath the covers as the thunder crashed, then silence. The boys heard a panther scream somewhere in the mountain, answered by the scream of a second panther. They thought that it sounded like the blood-curdling screams of a woman.

Last spring, the boys' cousin, Sally Jane, moved into a cabin just up the road from the boys with her mama, Aunt Olive. Sally Jane is the same age as Luke. She also watched the lightning in her bedroom and heard the panthers scream. Just like the boys, Sally Jane thought the sound of the panther's scream was an exciting part of mountain life.

World War II was over and things had settled down across the nation as well as up on the ridge. Times were improving for everyone. The ridge on Panther Creek Mountain was a community of half a dozen families of modest means. They did not have electricity or running water in their homes. In the evenings the kids read by the light of oil lamps and used outhouses when they had to go to the bathroom.

Once a week everyone in the family took baths in a big galvanized laundry tub near the wood-burning stove in the kitchen. The water came from the spring up on the hill behind the cabin.

The kids were on their own during the summers. They spent the days in their tree house, exploring the woods, streams, caves and the ponds, as well as river rafting. Every day was an adventure for Clay, Luke and Sally Jane as they experienced the wonders of living on an Appalachian Mountain Ridge in 1951.

Come along and join them as school ends and summer begins for the kids on Panther Creek Mountain.

Clyde McCulley, author

CHAPTER 1

HURRAY! SCHOOL'S OUT FOR THE SUMMER!

"School's out for the summer!" shouted the kids of the Wild Cat Valley School. They all said goodbye to their teachers and dashed out to get on their school buses.

For Clay and Luke, summer days meant going without shoes, playing in the woods and creeks, and making discoveries. They could not wait for the old yellow school bus to drop them off at Panther Creek Road.

When the bus finally stopped at their road, the boys jumped off and kicked off their shoes. They felt the warm sand between their toes. Each boy had a big grin on his face. They loved going barefoot.

"I will race you up the road to our cabin," said Luke, as he took off.

Clay knew he could not let his little brother beat him home, so he started to run, then spied Luke's shoes on the road where Luke had kicked them off.

"You may beat me, but you're going to have to come all the way back down from the ridge to get your shoes," yelled Clay.

Luke came to a quick stop.

'How did I forget my shoes?!' he fumed to himself, and reluctantly returned to get them.

Clay laughed and laughed, which only made Luke fume even more.

When Luke came back to get his shoes, Clay tore off running and beat Luke home.

"No fair!" yelled Luke, but Clay only laughed again.

When they entered the cabin, they could smell sugar cookies, fresh from the oven.

Mama grinned at the boys, knowing that it was good for them to have summer recess from school.

Both boys beamed and said that they loved school, but it was great for summer to arrive. Here in the woods, they felt that they got a "real" education!

Mama smiled and gave each boy a glass of buttermilk and three sugar cookies.

After their snack, they took a notebook and pencil and walked up to the water spring where they could sit on the log bench and make their summer plans. They wrote the following lists:

A. Summer Adventures
Camping
River rafting
Swimming
Kite Flying
Biking
Fishing
Indian Arrow Head hunting
Build a Tree house,
and....Unknown Adventures

B. Money Making Ideas
Pick up cold drink bottles along the road and sell them.
Sell Wild Plums
Sell Watermelons
Sell Flower and Vegetable Seeds
And...Unknown Money Making Ideas

C. Family Chores
Feed chickens
Feed Hogs

Feed Smokey and old cow
Help Mama wash clothes on Wednesdays
Wash dishes at suppertime
And....Unknown chores

D. Anything else we haven't thought of....

"I think that should be enough to get the summer started," said Clay.

"You think we can do all that in one summer?"

"Yeah, I think so—We'll fill our days with fun. I really want to build a tree house and maybe a small log cabin."

"A log cabin? News to me! When did you think of that, Clay?"

"Oh, one night after you went to sleep and I was lying awake listening to see if the panther up in the mountain would scream. All of a sudden I thought, why don't we build a real miniature log cabin, just big enough for the two of us to get in? Luke said, "Well, what about Georgie or other friends? It should be big enough for them too."

Clay agreed and said that they could go into the pine forest and cut a lot of small trees to build walls high enough for them to stand up in.

"That sounds like a lot of work," said Luke. "Let's start with some of our other plans first."

"Okay, but we should aim for building a log cabin at some point."

They climbed the ladder to the attic that night and both had trouble getting to sleep because of the exciting possibilities that lay ahead.

Luke finally drifted off to sleep and Clay heard two panthers scream in the wild woods up in the mountain above their cabin.

Clay loved the sound, but it also scared him.

He was excited knowing that they lived in the mountains, something that most boys could only imagine in their wildest dreams.

CHAPTER 2

BUILDING A TREE HOUSE

Clay and Luke had a favorite tree that hung from the cliff overlooking the valley below. Its roots grew into the cliff, allowing the tree to practically hang in midair.

On the first day of summer break, they decided to build a tree house. The tree had large limbs that grew perfectly for supporting it—limbs that grew straight out over the cliff, making it easy to build a floor.

The thought of it excited them. "We will probably have one of the only tree houses in the world that hangs out over a high and dangerous cliff."

They searched around the community and through the woods gathering up old boards that people had discarded. Pa gave them a can of nails and the tools they needed; a saw, hammer, and some rope.

The first thing they did was to cut boards just the right length for steps, which they nailed to the trunk of the tree so they could climb up and down. Next, they wrapped long boards together with part of the rope. Clay climbed the steps and instructed Luke to push the pile of boards as high up the tree as he could. Clay hoisted the boards up so they could lay them across the limbs.

They worked all morning and by lunchtime had built a platform about eight by eight feet square. They were delighted! They stood up and looked out across the valley with the binoculars they had purchased at the Army Surplus store in town. It was amazing how different the valley looked by being only 15 feet higher in the air.

As they stood up, Luke looked down to the cliffs below and almost felt dizzy. "Man, oh man, this is high, high, high!" he shouted. His eyes grew big and round.

Clay laughed, "You had better be careful and not fall, because you would look like melted butter spread on the rocks below."

Luke laughed and turned a funny shade of green. He wanted to quickly build the walls of the house so he and his brother wouldn't fall off.

By the end of the second day they had completed the walls, and had an old tin roof built the day after that. They thought they should invite their friend Georgie Robinson over to see their new 'Headquarters'—They thought he would be impressed and possibly a little jealous too. They also wanted to bring Mama and Pa and have them climb up into it.

"Mama will be scared to death—You know she hates heights," said Luke.

Luke had an idea. "Why don't we spread the word around the cabins here on the ridge that for a nickel, kids can climb up into our tree house and get a fabulous view of the Great Smoky Mountains. I think they will love it! We will make some money to buy new bicycles."

"Great idea! You are a genius, Luke!"

9

They told all of the neighbors. Soon five boys and three girls crowded around the tree trunk. They were anxious to see the new tree house and get a good view of the Smokies.

Pa and Mama came down to watch. Mama said it was best for the five boys to climb up first, and then the girls climb up after the boys.

"Oh, I get it," said one of the boys. "That way we can't see the girls bloomers, because we will already be up in the tree house."

"You got it," said Mama, "AND, the girls come down first."

They all paid their nickel admission and were thrilled by the height and amazed by the view of the Smoky Mountains.

The tree house had been a success and would be Clay and Luke's favorite hangout for years to come.

That night, as they lay in their bed up in the attic, Luke was concerned. He hoped the panther would never find the tree house.

Clay laughed and started to answer, but Luke was already asleep.

Soon the panther let out her blood-curdling scream. Clay smiled at the sound in the darkness, rolled over and fell asleep.

CHAPTER 3

CLAY AND LUKE MAKE A BIG DISCOVERY

When Clay and Luke headed out for the day, it was already getting hot.

Clay suggested that they ride their bikes a few miles north and explore Panther Creek. Luke thought it was a good idea.

They went to the shed and found their backpacks from the Army surplus store in town. They went into the kitchen and made peanut butter and banana sandwiches. They also packed graham crackers, green apples from Granny Palmer's tree, and a jar full of wild red plums, which they had just picked. Finally, they filled their canteens with fresh brewed sweet tea.

"This should hold us over for the day, unless we get lost," Luke joked.

The two boys never got lost. They each had a good sense of direction.

Their parents were not at home, so they left a note saying that they were headed north to look for the creek they had found last year, and they would be home by supper time.

They jumped on their bikes and headed up Panther Creek Road.

Clay rode ahead of Luke, and yelled back, "I hope we can remember where the creek goes under the road. I remember there were a lot of bushes along that spot. We did not even realize that it was there and stumbled upon it when you had to stop and pee!"

Luke laughed, remembering that he was going to pee on the road because no one was around, but Clay thought someone might be hiding somewhere and watching. That spooked Luke.

Clay let him know that he was only joking, that he was just trying to make him go into the bushes to pee.

But that had turned out great because they discovered the big creek under all that brush and it had all been because of Luke.

They had ridden for about half an hour, when they saw a dip in the road and realized that they were at the right place.

They slowed down and watched for moving water.

"Stop talking, and listen." said Clay. "Maybe we can hear the water running."

They got off their bikes and listened, and sure enough, they heard the creek quite clearly.

"We have no idea who owns this land," said Luke. "It's probably someone who lives in town, because I have never heard any of the neighbors talking about any country people having land up here."

"Well, I don't see any 'No Trespassing' signs, so I say it belongs to us for today!" said Clay.

"You got that right, man."

They wanted to hide their bikes so no one would take them. After dragging them through the bushes and hiding them under the bridge, they knew no one would find them.

After the bikes were well hidden, the boys started to wade through the water in the creek. The bushes were too close to the water for them to be able to walk on the bank. Soon, the woods opened up and the bushes were back from the creek and they could see a long way up the rocky stream bottom.

"Ding-dang, this is beautiful! Look how clear the water is," said Clay.

They both got on their bellies, and scooped up the clear cold water in their hands to drink. "This is great tasting water, even if it does have fish and frogs and snakes in it," said Clay. Luke gulped. Clay went on, "These critters won't hurt us, just think of Davy Crockett and Daniel Boone traveling for days through the woods. They didn't have wells or springs to drink from. They drank from creeks and rivers, and they lived!" Luke felt better hearing this.

As they got up from the creek and started to walk again, they heard a terrifying scream that sounded like a woman screaming. They both froze in place, and Luke's eyes got as big as watermelons.

"Clay, what was that? Sounds like a woman is being murdered!" whispered Luke.

Clay was shaken too, but he thought for a minute and said, "Luke, I am quite sure that was a panther screaming. The neighbors say there are panthers up in these woods. I have laid in bed at night and heard them screaming away off in the distance." Luke wanted to turn around and head home.

Clay told him that panthers are afraid of humans and will only attack if the are cornered or if they have their young with them, so they were okay, and to just keep going.

Now they both kept their eyes open.

As they walked along the bank of the creek, they could see small fish swimming—a lot of them.

Clay said it was too bad that they didn't bring fishing poles with them, that if they had they could catch some fish, build a fire and have a great meal.

Luke wanted to know if Clay knew how to clean fish and get them ready to cook.

He said he thought they could figure that out and if nothing else, just cut off the heads and tails and cook them over the fire.

"Did you bring matches?" Luke asked.

"Of course, I did, what if we got lost and we were here for days until someone found us. We would need matches to build a fire at night to keep the panthers away," said Clay.

"Now you are trying to scare me, so just stop it!"

"Okay, Okay, I will. Sorry."

They were about a mile and a half from where they left the bikes when they heard something running fast through the nearby bushes. They both froze and crouched low to hide and see what it was.

A large rabbit came running by them at full speed, with a fox close behind. The rabbit did not see the boys, but the fox did and he turned and ran the opposite direction.

The boys started running after the rabbit, and all of a sudden it disappeared.

The boys stopped, a bit bewildered and then got down close to the ground to see where it went. As they crawled, they fell forward into a large hole they hadn't seen. The large opening was totally filled with grown pine trees and bushes, and the limbs of the trees had hidden the opening to a cave! It had looked like flat land to the boys.

Neither of them was hurt. They stood up and started to look around, but it was quite dark in this place. As their eyes adjusted, they realized that they were in the opening of a large cave with a stone ceiling.

They looked around, and realized that there had been people in this space before them, but it looked like many years ago. They found strange things, objects made of metal. There were old pots, pans, an old copper tub and an old wooden table. Nearby was a fire pit made out of stone. Next to it was a bubbling spring of clear cold water.

"What is this place?" said Luke, "Have we found some kind of old torture chamber or something? I am not sure I want to be here. Let's go!"

"No, no," said Clay, "I think I have figured it out. Maybe we have found a place where people used to camp, probably back in the 1930s after the Depression. There are stories of bank robbers who hid out in the hills away from the lawmen. They probably hid here for days, cooked their food over the fire pit, and slept here on blankets. The cave would protect them from the weather and also hide them. I wonder if they hid any of the stolen money here?"

They went back to the entrance and pulled the limbs back over the opening to disguise it in case anyone else came by.

When they went back in, they discovered a small hole in the stone ceiling above them where smoke could escape without filling the cave.

"We have found something very, very special," exclaimed Clay. "Obviously, none of the people in these parts know about this or we would have heard about it. The old copper is probably worth a lot of money. This simply means that you and I have found a place of our very own, our 'secret club house' and we cannot tell a living soul about it. Do you understand what I am saying, Luke? It is our secret hideaway forever!"

Again, Luke's eyes grew huge with a look of fear, surprise, and excitement!

"Okay, I agree. We don't tell anybody! Does that even mean our good friend Georgie?"

"That even means Georgie. Cross your heart and hope to die, stick a needle in your eye if you tell anybody?"

Luke crossed his heart that he would not tell.

They cleaned the cave. There were pine needles that had blown in, all over the floor of the "new room".

Clay thought the needles would make a great bed. They picked them up and piled them into two beds.

They were starting to get hungry, so they unpacked the peanut butter and banana sandwiches, and cut up the green apples with their pocketknives. They opened the canteens and drank the wonderful sweet tea that Mama made.

"Let's build a small fire in the old fire pit," said Luke.

"Okay, but we need to keep it small because we don't want someone to see the smoke and discover us."

They filled the old bucket with water, ready to douse the fire quickly if needed. Then they gathered dry twigs and pine needles to build a fire. The burning pine needles smelled good to the boys. They lay down on the new beds end watched the fire. Both drifted off to sleep. The fire burned itself out. They must have slept for about an hour. All of a sudden they were awakened by the blast of a shotgun!

Luke grabbed Clay and whispered, "Someone is going to kill us!"

"Quiet!" whispered Clay.

Their hearts were beating a hundred miles per hour! They could hear the voices of two men, maybe three. One of them was saying, "Where did that damn rabbit go? He disappeared."

Clay and Luke looked toward the opening and saw a rabbit crouching and trembling. One of the men said, "I think he went into a hole over here." All of a sudden there was another blast of the gun, but this time it was aimed at the opening and they saw pine needles flying.

Both boys were really frightened now.

They hoped the men would not get down on their hands and knees and discover the secret opening. They were afraid that if the men found them, they would be in big trouble.

Luke whispered, "What if they are bad men, who kidnap kids and sell them as slaves?"

Clay almost laughed, but he was too scared.

One of the men yelled, "Come on, let's go. I'm sure there are other rabbits around." "No, let's try to find the one we shot at," said the man who sounded like he was closer to the "entrance."

Finally the men gave up and left. The boys could hear their voices trailing off as they left the area.

"Thank the good Lord they did not have coon dogs with them," said Clay. "If they did, those dogs would have followed that rabbit right into our secret place. They would have discovered us, too, and then you know what a howl they would have made, and possibly attacked us!"

Again Luke's eyes grew wide. Clay thought to himself, "If I don't stop scaring Luke, his eyes might pop right out of his head."

He giggled and Luke wanted to know what he was giggling about.

"Oh, nothing."

After the men were well out of sight, the boys went over to see where the shotgun blast hit the opening. Pine needles were torn from the trees, but they did not find a dead rabbit. He must have escaped. They were glad about that and sighed a long sigh of relief.

They sat on the ground in the secret cave and tried to relive what had just happened. They talked about whether it was too dangerous to be there, but then decided that they were definitely going to return.

They had no idea if the men usually hunted in these parts regularly, or if this happened to be their first time.

If the hunters were to return, the boys would have to have a system in place that would warn them. They would go back home and work out a plan.

They left the hideout, being sure to hide the entrance by covering it with tree limbs and old brush. They followed the creek back the mile and a half towards the road and their bikes. They were quiet for a while, always listening to see if they could hear the men's voices, or shots being fired. After about forty minutes, they spotted the road, got the bikes out from under the bridge and headed down Panther Creek Road.

As they neared home, both looked at each other. Both understood they could never talk with anyone about the secret cave.

CHAPTER 4
WE HAVE TO MAKE A PLAN!

Mama had supper almost ready as they came through the back door. They could smell the potatoes frying in the big iron skillet, the cornbread and an apple pie, which had just come from the oven.

Mama wanted to know about their day's adventures.

They both looked at each other as though she already knew about their day, but then they realized there was no way she could know.

They told her that they had a pretty thrilling day, chased a rabbit (but could not catch it) and played in a wonderful creek that they found.

Luke's eyes were big again, but he didn't say a word.

After supper, they washed the dishes for Mama as they did each night. After the dishes were done, the boys went out into yard to watch fireflies and talk quietly about the hideout. Even though it was now dark, the air was still hot and sticky.

"Luke, I have been thinking about what we can do that will warn us if someone is approaching our hideout. We have to have a warning rigged up far enough away from the cave entrance so that if we hear the alarm we will have time to put out our fire.

It's lucky that the water spring is right beside the fire pit, so we can keep a bucket full of water to quickly douse the fire if we need to."

They tried to think about what type of alarm they could use.

They realized that they couldn't have a bell or anything like that that would let the hunters know that anyone was nearby. It had to be an alarm that the hunters would not realize had been tripped. They remembered that Pa had a lot of old fishing line that he never used. They could tie it from one tree to another, low to the ground, all the way around our cave. If the hunters got too close, they would trip it and cause a piece of dead tree trunk to fall, signaling them that the enemy was approaching.

When the boys heard the falling tree trunk, the hunters would too, but they would think that it just happened naturally. When the boys heard the tree fall, they would quickly douse the fire and huddle in the corner of the cave in case the hunters fired the shotgun.

Luke's eyes grew big again as he whispered, "Maybe we should just forget we ever found our secret hideout. Let's just pretend that it was a bad dream."

"Are you kidding? This is the kind of thing that you read about in Tom Sawyer and Huck Finn! Most boys never ever have a chance to know the thrill of doing this kind of thing. This is the stuff they write books about. Luke, maybe someday we will write our own book about Clay and Luke's adventures. Our adventures are just as exciting as Tom and Huck's, maybe even better."

They had a lot of trouble going to sleep that night. After a while, Luke said, "Clay, are you still awake?"

"Yeah, why?"

"Well what if those hunters come into our secret place and shoot us dead?"

"They won't. Now go to sleep and don't have a nightmare. If you listen closely, you may hear the panthers screaming up in the woods."

"Okay," said Luke, and then he fell asleep and promptly started to snore before he could hear the panther.

Clay lay awake and heard a panther scream twice before he drifted off.

The next morning they awoke to wonderful smells coming from Mama's kitchen. They smelled biscuits in the oven, eggs frying, and fried apple pies, their very favorite.

"So, what are you boys going to do for an adventure today?" asked Pa as Mama served the boys their breakfast.

"We will probably go back up into the woods."

Then Clay asked, "Pa, do our lives ever sound kind of like Tom Sawyer and Huck Finn?"

Luke's eyes grew bigger.

"Oh, I think you boys have much more exciting lives than they did."

Both boys laughed. "I told you, Luke," said Clay.

They enjoyed breakfast. Luke was smacking his lips and Clay told him that it's not polite to eat like that. Luke looked at him, and said, "I love Mama's cooking and will smack if I want too."

Mama told them to not pester each other, so they stopped. Mama smiled.

The boys each took a bucket of feed and went to the old barn to feed Smokey, their old horse. While they were gone, Mama heated a teakettle of water on the stove, so the boys could wash the dishes when they returned.

After the dishes were done, Clay asked, "Pa, could Luke and I have some of that old fishing line that you found at the town dump a while back?"

"Sure, I guess so. What are you planning to do now?"

"We want to do some experimenting with it in the woods. Perhaps we can figure out a way to catch birds, or maybe something else?" The boys looked at each other, knowing that it was "something else" that they were intending to do with Pa's fishing line.

"You boys never cease to amaze me," Pa smiled and said, "Use what you need."

"Thanks!"

The boys went up the path to the old shed behind their cabin and found the fishing line. It was clear. They yanked on it and found that it was very strong. Since it was clear, one could hardly see it.

"Perfect," said clay. "This should do the trick." They put the rolls of fishing line and a flashlight in an old gunnysack, and started to get on their bikes.

"Wait!" Luke said, "We have not made any sandwiches for lunch!"

"Oh, yeah, good thinking."

So a few minutes later, they had sandwiches, two apples, plums and sweet tea. They put them into old army backpacks and were off to their secret hideaway. The boys were excited (and a little bit scared, too.)

As they approached the cave entrance, they looked carefully to see if anyone had been around the cave. They found the tree limbs that they had used to cover the entrance were exactly as they had left them. They pulled the branches away and shined their flashlight inside to see if there were any animals in the cave. They watched for eyes beaming back at them, but they saw none, and that made them feel much better.

They took their backpacks into the cave and sat them on an old table that the "bank robbers" left. They then went back outside. They took out Pa's fishing line and started attaching it to tree trunks down near the ground. They found old pieces of fallen trees and tied the line to them, then hoisted them into position against standing trees, so they would fall and warn the boys if the fishing line was tripped.

They found that they could take strong tree limbs and using leverage under the larger pieces of trees, lift them into place.

In order to do this, they had to put a strong tree limb under the old pieces and put all their body weight on it to lift the old pieces up against live trees and tie the line to them.

The trees were very heavy, especially for Luke, but he was a good sport.

Clay said, "Now we have to try out our warning system and see if it works.

They started walking through the trees and when their feet hit the fishing line, an old tree trunk near them fell. It made a hugh crash!

"It worked," they both yelled, "Yipeee!"

Then Luke got one of those looks on his face. "This means we now have to lift that old tree back up again!"

"Yes, we do, but we proved that our warning system works, Luke!"

They were both delighted. The tree did not seem as heavy to hoist as it did the first time.

"Now we can feel safe in our hideout, even when we spend the night," Clay said.

"Spend the night!" exclaimed Luke, "Are we really going to sleep in the cave at night?" His eyes got as big as two full moons.

"But what about the screaming panthers? They will eat us alive!"

"Don't worry," said Clay, "remember our warning system will let us known if an enemy approaches."

"But what if a panther is up in the trees and jumping from to tree to another and does not trip our alarm?" said big-eyed Luke.

"Panthers stay on the ground, I am pretty sure, so don't worry about it," said Clay.

"But what happens if they avoid our alarm and we wake up in the night and see a panther in the entrance to our cave? THEN what are we going to do to keep from getting eaten?" asked Luke with a trembling voice.

"Stay calm, I have been thinking about how to handle it if that happens. You know the old large metal pan we found by the fire pit? Well, we are going to get a big stick and see how loud a sound it makes when you hit the pan with it. If it's loud enough, it will scare the daylights out of anybody or anything. Lets go in the cave and try it.

Clay took the stick and Luke held the pan while he slammed it. It made a really loud ringing sound.

"Now tell me, Luke, if you were a panther and came sneaking into this cave in the dark and suddenly you heard that loud ringing sound, what would you do?"

Luke thought for a minute and said, "I would probably pee my pants."

"Well panthers don't have pants, but I am sure he would run like crazy!" said Clay.

"And probably pee down its legs as it ran!" shouted Luke. They both laughed.

The boys built a fire and watched the flames flicker as they ate the sandwiches, plums and apples. They took a short nap on the pine needle beds. When they awoke, the fire had burned out. They poured water from the spring on the smoldering cinders and started packing to head back home.

As they left the cave, Luke said, "Remember, where we put the fishing line around the trees so we don't trip it."

"Right, or we will have to set the booby trap again."

It bothered each of them that they had kept the cave a secret from Mama and Pa, so about a week later, they decided that it was time to tell them about the cave.

They had also done a lot of thinking and talking about spending the night there, trying to build up their courage.

During supper, they told Pa and Mama about discovering the cave, about their theory that it was a bank robber's hideout, and how they set up a warning system and tested it, so they thought they would be safe. They also told about banging a pan if anything tried to enter the cave.

They asked Pa if he would like to join them for an overnight adventure in a secret cave. He did not answer. He said that he wanted to know where the boys found a cave. He had lived here many years and did not know of any secret cave in these parts. They explained in detail how they had seen a rabbit being chased by a fox and they followed the rabbit and discovered the cave.

Pa said he was a little concerned about the boys staying overnight. "You know you are going to be way back in the hills and I want you to be safe."

Mama said, "So it sounds like you boys have been planning this for a while, huh?"

"Yes, Mama, we have, but we did not want to worry you and Pa," said Clay.

Luke sat there and said nothing.

Pa noticed and said, "Now Luke, are you alright with this overnight plan?"

Luke looked at Clay, then at Pa and said, "If Clay thinks it is safe, then I am okay with it."

Mama had a worried look on her face.

Again, they asked Pa if he would like to camp in the hideout with them. He said, no. He thought that they were old enough to camp alone, but he would like for them to take the .22 rifle with them. He reminded Luke that it was only Clay who was old enough to use the gun.

Both boys agreed, shaking their heads that they understood. They said they would probably wait a few more weeks before staying overnight.

Mama was relieved.

CHAPTER 5

DISCOVERING THE CRAZY WILD WOMAN

Pa grew a few grapevines up the trail behind the cabin in a little field he had cleared in the woods. The grapevines were close to an old shed where Luke and Clay liked to play. They called it their "Clubhouse."

They used ideas from the Boy Scout handbooks that they had checked out from the library to make their own "boy scout" room in the "clubhouse." They did not have money to buy the uniforms required to join the real Boy Scouts. They also did not have a way to get to town at night when the scouts had their meetings because the family did not have a car.

Even though the old shed was rickety and just about falling down, they loved having their very own clubhouse.

It was a hot summer morning. Mama was home and Pa had walked down the mountain to town. The boys thought they would spend the morning swimming in old man Gerber's pond and try to catch a few fish.

They got the cane poles and fish hooks out from under the cabin.

Luke said, "We should catch some grasshoppers for bait before we go."

They got out an old bedspread and each of the boys held two corners, one high and one low, near the ground. They held on tight and ran through the tall grass for about 100 feet before stopping. Then they pulled the lower part of the bedspread up high and held it together at the top so the grasshoppers could not jump out.

Carefully they unfolded it. There were dozens of grasshoppers, green ones and black ones and every size you could think of.

"Man, oh man, we did good," said Clay. "We have at least a hundred juicy grasshoppers."

They grabbed them one by one and put them into an old canning jar, then closed the lid.

They thought with a little luck they might be able to bring Mama a mess of fish for supper. They knew she would like that.

They were excited and ran to the pond.

The pond water was warm from the morning sun, so they stripped off their clothes and swam bare-naked for a while. They tried to see how long they could hold their breath under water. There was a large rock sticking out of the water and they took turns diving off the rock.

After a while, Luke said, "We had better see if we can catch a few fish—It *is* almost noon."

They excitedly opened the jar, took out two large grasshoppers and pushed the fishhook through the grasshopper's bodies. The grasshoppers were kicking and squirming as they threw the line into the water.

Within seconds, each had a bite. They struggled to pull their catch onto the bank of the pond. To their amazement, two large bass lay flopping on the bank.

"Wow!" said Luke. His eyes grew big.

"Did you bring that old bucket to put the fish in?"

He just looked at Clay and said, "Was I supposed too?" They both laughed.

The two large bass would be all they needed for supper.

They both suddenly realized they'd been fishing bare-naked, and laughed as they put their clothes on. After finding an old gunnysack to carry the fish home, they headed back down to the house for dinner at 12:00 sharp, as Mama asked them to do.

When they went into the house to eat, Mama seemed upset and very nervous. Luke and Clay looked at each other. They knew something was really wrong. They asked her what was upsetting her.

She did not want to say, so they asked if someone was dead, or had been killed.

She said, "No, nothing like that."

Clay said, "Please tell us then."

She just said she had to think about what she should do.

"You boys go on back up to the pond and fish some more."

They put the fish in a tub of fresh spring water to keep for supper, then ate. After dinner, they headed out the back door to go back to the pond, as Mama had requested them to do.

Clay thought that instead of going back to the pond, they should play in the grape vineyard and stay near the house because of the strange way Mama was acting.

They went up the trail to the little vineyard, and picked grapes as they had done many times before. They decided to go into their "clubhouse." Clay put his hand on the door handle, and started to pull the door open. All of a sudden they heard a woman's horrifying scream, then more screaming and crying coming from the shed.

Both boys froze in their tracks. They could not move. They were scared to death. Luke grabbed Clay and held on to him for dear life. Clay told him to let go, so he could open the door a little more and see what on earth was happening.

Luke begged Clay not to open the door.

Clay was scared too. "But the woman, whoever she is, is crying." he said, "We have to open it, Luke, she must be hurt."

Luke was still frozen with fear.

Mama heard the screaming and came running as fast as she could. She yelled at the boys, "I thought you two were up at the pond! Go down to the cabin, NOW!"

But it was too late. Clay had pulled the door open. There was a woman curled up in the corner, wrapped in an old blanket and crying. She had wild white hair and scary eyes. He did not know what to do.

Mama pushed the boys aside. She went over to the scary looking woman and took her in her arms and said, "Boys, this is Aunt June. She is Aunt Olive's sister and mine. She came here because she had nowhere else to go. She is a patient in the Eastern State Mental Hospital. She escaped last night, caught a ride to our house and hid here in the shed.

"After you boys went to the pond, I heard something up here in the shed. When I checked, I found Aunt June. Thank goodness Pa had already gone to town when I found her. He would not want her here."

She told the boys she was sorry that she had not told them about her before. She thought she would always be in the hospital and that they would never find out about her. She told them, "Aunt June is very sick, but she does know who I am and she trusts me."

"You don't need to be afraid of her,—She only screamed because she was frightened when she heard the shed door open. She was afraid that it was the state hospital people coming to take her back," Mama said.

She continued, "The hospital knows our address and that I am her next of kin, so I am sure they will send someone to get her soon."

This is unreal, thought Luke and Clay. Luke's eyes were bulging. They did not know anything about an

Aunt June, and now they were told this screaming woman with wild white hair and scary eyes was their aunt!

Mama told them to go to the bluff and watch for the ambulance and to come back and let her know when they spotted it. A few minutes later, they looked down to the valley and saw dust flying from a big white ambulance speeding up the dusty dirt road. They ran to tell Mama.

As it pulled up to the cabin, the boys saw a big Red Cross on the doors and the words "Eastern State Hospital." The ambulance had two men and two women inside. They got out of the ambulance with doctor's bags and something white. They asked the boys and Mama to please get out of the way. Mama begged them to please to be kind to her. One of the hospital women assured Mama that they would be gentle with Aunt June. They tied her hands and feet with soft gauze to the ambulance stretcher and gave her a shot in her arm. In a few minutes, she stopped screaming and settled down.

Just as they were loading her into the ambulance, Pa came running up. "What's going on here?" he demanded. They could see Mama had been dreading Pa's return from town. He did not know about Aunt June's escape from the hospital.

Mama went over to the ambulance to try to tell Aunt June that she loved her, but the shot they gave to her had already put her to sleep. Luke and Clay tried to slip around to the other side to see inside the ambulance, and to get another peek at Aunt June.

They watched as the big white ambulance pulled away from the cabin. Neighbors from the ridge gathered around. Clay realized that they were thinking that someone in his family had gone mad when they saw the State Hospital ambulance.

Luke and Clay could hardly breathe.

Luke wanted to know all about Aunt June. "Who is she, and does this mean that we're also going to have to go to the mental hospital someday since she's our aunt?"

Mama told the boys that they didn't have to worry.

Luke said, "Okay" but there was still fear in his eyes.

That afternoon they all sat on the shady side of the cabin and tried to sort out everything they had witnessed. Mama felt terrible that the boys had discovered Aunt June in "their" clubhouse.

Pa was still fuming about "the boys being exposed to all this mess."

Finally everyone settled down. Mama made some sweet tea and everyone sat and fanned themselves with cardboard fans.

Clay told Luke that they should go back to old man Gerber's pond for another swim. He hoped Luke would not have nightmares over this. He turned nine years old only three months ago. This had been a lot for a nine-year old.

Clay thought, "Thank goodness that I am eleven, but I'm not sure that I'm ready for this experience, either."

Aunt June died a short time later in the State Hospital. Mama, Pa, Aunt Olive and their older brother, Uncle Frank from Memphis, claimed her body for burial. No one else attended.

After that time the boys always called it Aunt June's shed. They never played in it again.

They started to gather old boards with the idea that some day they would build a new Clubhouse, but they would put a lock on the door.

It was a restless night for Clay and Luke. The panthers let out their screams, but Clay and Luke did not hear them. Exhausted, they had already fallen asleep.

CHAPTER 6
CLAY WINS THE GAME

Clay squinted his eyes awake early one morning. The sun was shining brightly through the cabin window in the boys' attic room.

"Hey Luke! It's summer, school is out and we're sleeping the day away! Get up now!"

Luke looked at him with sleepy eyes. He knew Clay was right. The last few days had been rainy, but today the sun lit up the sky.

Mama had gone into town to work and Pa had gone to talk with a man about buying a mule to help him pull cut timber out of the woods. The man's house was about two miles away, and Pa had to walk.

The boys went out into the yard, rolled up their pants, and splashed around in the puddles. Summer was the time to go barefoot all day and wiggle your toes in the grass. By the end of summer the boy's feet were as tough as shoe leather. They could walk on any stony path, through any rocky stream or on the pinecones and pine needles on the forest floor. They loved it!

Luke asked, "Do you have any ideas for today's adventures?"

"Well," Clay said, "Since it's not raining, I was thinking about going up to the woods and swinging on the old muscadine vine out over the creek."

Luke thought that was a great idea—he loved flying out over the creek. Sometimes they would let go of the vine and drop into the deep, cool water below.

They packed biscuits, red and yellow plums, berries and muscadines for breakfast.

Luke could already taste them.

They often ate in the woods, because it was much more fun than eating in the hot summer kitchen at home. Mama had roasted fresh peanuts in the shell before going to work and they were still warm. Luke grabbed a bag to eat along the way.

As they hiked up the trail to the woods, they passed a cabin where a water well was being dug. No one was yet living in the cabin. Tory Smitters was hired to dig the well and he had already dug down about ten feet.

After the rain had started, it had rained for three days straight, and hadn't dried out around the top of the well enough for him to start digging again.

Tory was a big strong boy, and not too bright according to Pa, but he had good common sense and was strong as an ox.

"Let's go over and have a look," Luke said.

There was no fencing around the well, so they could walk right over and peer down into it. There was already quite a bit of water in the well from the recent rain.

Clay suggested that they play a game of going around and around the well to see who could get closest to the edge with out falling in.

Luke looked at him for a few seconds. He did not want to look like a coward, so he agreed but he didn't want to get too close. He was sure there were poisonous snakes down there.

Clay set the lunch bag on the ground. They circled around and around the opening of the well. It was fun and they were both laughing with excitement. All of a sudden, Luke's foot slipped on the damp clay and he started to fall. He tried to grab a small bush growing at the edge of the well, but it did not hold. He fell screaming down the well and into the muddy water. He made a terrible splash. He struggled to stand up in the water.

He yelled, "Clay, this is all your fault! Get me out NOW!"

"Are you hurt?"

"No, I don't think so but I am sure there are snakes down here. Get me out!" screamed Luke.

Clay looked around for a rope, but Tory had taken it home with him along with the shovel and the bucket. "I don't have anything to pull you out with, Luke, and I don't think I'm strong enough to pull you up even if I did have a rope. Tory is not around, so I will run up the hill and see if Mrs. Robinson can help us. She is always home."

"Hurry!" yelled Luke. He was mad!

Clay shot like a bullet for the Robinson's cabin.

Clay shouted as he ran into the Robinsons' front yard, "Luke fell in the well! Come and help me get him out!"

Mrs. Robinson ran out of the house and looked at Clay. She was very cross-eyed, so she looked first out of her blue eye and then out of the brown one. Because of her first name and her one blue eye, she'd been nicknamed "Bonnie Blue."

"What are you saying, boy?" she exclaimed.

Clay yelled again, "Luke is down in the water at the bottom of the well!"

Georgie came running around the corner of the cabin, his eyes as big as cow pies.

Bonnie Blue yelled for Georgie to get two ropes. They all three ran as fast as they could down the hill towards the well.

As they got near the well they could hear Luke yelling out a prayer: "LORD, SAVE ME FROM THE WICKED SNAKES THAT ARE IN THIS WELL!"

Clay thought, "He thinks that he needs to yell because he is so far down in the well that the Lord might not be able to hear him." It was funny, but Clay was too worried to laugh.

Bonnie Blue, Georgie and Clay all ran to the edge. They lay on their bellies and tried to reassure Luke that they were going to save him, but he was starting to cry. Clay tried to tell him that there were no snakes in the well.

Bonnie Blue made a loop in the rope and tied a knot in it so Luke could put his foot inside it.

She dropped the rope down in the well and said, "Boy, you stop that crying and listen to me."

When Luke finally calmed down, Bonnie Blue told him to put one foot into the loop and stand up, then grab the rope with his hands and try to get his balance.

Luke did as he was told. They all pulled on the rope, together, but there was a problem. Since it rained for several days the clay around the well was slick and they all started to slide towards the edge.

Bonnie Blue yelled for them to stop!

They had pulled Luke up to where he was about two feet above the water, and he started yelling, "DON'T STOP NOW! THERE ARE SNAKES TRYING TO GET ME. I AM SURE OF IT!"

Bonnie Blue looked at Clay and Georgie out of one crossed eye, and then the other. "Help us, Jesus!" is all she said.

She thought for a minute and yelled to Clay, "Get that other rope and tie it to that small tree over yonder and tie the other end of it around my waist."

She and Georgie were trying to hold Luke above the water without sliding in themselves.

Clay hurried and did as he was told. Now Bonnie Blue could not slide in.

She told Georgie and Clay "You two get on drier ground and grab hold of the rope between me and the tree and every time I yell 'PULL!', you pull for all you are worth." So when she yelled "PULL!", they pulled Bonnie Blue and she pulled Luke.

Luke was whimpering. He was only nine years old, so Clay thought it was okay for him to whimper. They all pulled and pulled. Finally they saw the top of his head, then his eyes. His eyes looked mad and scared. The three kept pulling until they had him up on the ground. They were all a mess, with mud all over them.

Clay asked Luke if any snakes bit him.

He said, "No, but I know they wanted to eat me alive." Then Luke realized that the bag got wet and the peanuts were all floating on the muddy water in the well. "Sorry."

"Its okay," Clay said.

Bonnie Blue sat down on the damp ground. Then she asked the question that Clay knew was coming: "Child, what on earth were you doing near that well?"

Clay tried to come up with a good answer that wouldn't sound stupid. Would Bonnie Blue believe it if he told her they were chasing a ball and didn't see the well, or perhaps that they lost their cat and wanted to see if it had fallen in the well and Luke slipped in? He did not want her to know they were playing a game to see who could get the closest to the edge as they went round and round the hole without falling in.

No, he knew he had to tell the truth. He told her that they had been playing a game and he'd won. He did not fall in the well.

Clay and Luke thanked Bonnie Blue and Georgie.

Bonnie Blue told Georgie, "You can't stay with them. You come home with me, boy, where it is safe."

Then she looked at Clay out of one eye, then the other. She did not say goodbye. Georgie was quiet. He and his mama just picked up their ropes and headed up the hill toward home.

Clay and Luke looked at each other, wondering what they were going to tell Mama when she asked why they were covered in mud. They would have to confess.

When the boys went to bed that night, they stayed quiet for a time, neither one saying anything.

Finally Clay could stand it no longer and said, "I am sorry, Luke. I thought it would be fun to play that stupid game. I had no idea you would fall in the well."

Luke lay there for a while and finally said, "Well, I am not sure that is really what you think, but I will have to say that the look on Bonnie Blue Robinson's face, when she looked at you, made up for all my fear."

They both laughed.

A few minutes later, the panther screamed and this time Luke heard it, too. He was having a little trouble going to sleep.

CHAPTER 7

DANGER! RAZORBACKS AHEAD

Clay and Luke were hiking on a narrow trail in the woods about a mile from their cabin. It was a place higher up the mountain where they did not often go. They were always aware that they needed to listen for the sounds of rattlesnakes. There were other poisonous snakes on the mountain, too; copperheads and cottonmouths, but they did not give warnings when humans were near, which made them the most scared. Pa always told them that the cottonmouth was the most dangerous one to watch for. They would stand their ground against a human and not back away, whereas copperheads were shyer and would try to get away.

Pa also said that animals consider the woods their home and humans as a potential enemy. "They are to be respected," he told them, "So always back away. Remember, they have a right to the woods."

The boys always kept this in mind when adventuring in the wild.

As they hiked along, Luke grabbed Clay. "What was that noise in the bushes? It sound like something big!"

Clay held up his hand as a signal for them to stop. They listened, and soon heard more rustling in the bushes, then grunting sounds.

The sounds got louder and all of a sudden, they saw something they had never seen before. It was a wild razorback pig, with huge tusks. Then they saw it was a mama with her three piglets.

The mama had not seen or heard Luke and Clay. They were downwind from the wild pigs, so she had not picked up their scent.

The boys had heard old men telling tales at the general store of razorbacks high in the mountains. And they knew that if the mama pig felt her piglets were in danger, she would charge the two of them.

Clay remembered what the old men had said, so he said to Luke, "If she turns toward us, run for those trees and get up one fast!"

Luke shook his head. His eyes were huge as always when he was scared. The two boys stayed perfectly still, neither making a move.

All of a sudden the mama pig spied the boys. She lowered her head and started to charge.

The boys tore out like lightning toward the trees, each one scaling a small tree, climbing high enough that the mama pig was not be able to gore them with her tusks.

"What do we do now?" shouted Luke.

"Just hang on and don't slip down the tree. Maybe she will leave in a few minutes—at least I hope!"

The pig circled around and around the trees under the boys; one tree and then the other one, snorting and rooting into the earth to let them know that they were her enemy. Then she would stop and look up at each of them and let out loud, blood-curdling grunt and squealing noises.

After what seemed like forever, she moved towards her piglets, who were staying back, looking frightened. The piglets had watched the whole thing. She snorted at them, then tore off running down the hill at full speed with the piglets trying to keep up with her.

After a while, Clay and Luke slid quietly down the trees. Neither said anything for few minutes, both as frightened as they had ever been.

Luke had tears in his eyes, but he did not want Clay to see them.

"Well, little brother, we were almost eaten alive."

Hearing Clay's words, he could not hold back the tears and started bawling.

Clay came over to comfort him, "You didn't pee your pants, did you?"

Both started to laugh and headed down the trail to the log cabin.

"Please don't tell anybody I cried, okay?"

"You know I would never do that, Luke. All that we're going to tell is what happened and how we bravely outsmarted that big old mama pig."

"Thanks Clay—I didn't mean to cry."

Clay understood.

During supper, they told Mama and Pa about their wild adventure. Mama looked a little frightened, but Pa just smiled and reminded them about the woods belonging to the animals and that the mama hog was letting them know that they were not welcomed. "You were both smart to climb a tree."

That night, the boys climbed the ladder to their beds in the attic. They lay awake talking about their narrow escape, reliving each scary moment.

Clay and Luke stayed awake to see if they could hear the panthers scream in the upper ridge. They listened for a while, and then Luke fell asleep.

A few minutes later, Clay heard the panther scream. He smiled and drifted off.

CHAPTER 8

NOT GOOD NEWS IN THE MAIL

Luke and Clay were always excited when the mailman, Old Joe, came up the mountain road in his old gray Nash car. They liked him because he always stopped to talk and wanted to know about their latest adventures. Pa always made fun of the mailman's car because he thought it looked like an old gray cast-iron bathtub turned upside down on four wheels.

One day the boys saw the car away off in the distance from their tree house.

They watched the car chugging up the mountain, then scurried down the tree and ran to the road to meet the mailman. He often had penny candy for each of them and they liked that.

Today, he greeted them with, "Hey fellas, it looks like I have a special letter for your Mama. It came from over on the other side of the mountain."

The boys looked at the return address and it was from Mrs. Olive Owens in Bear Creek, Tennessee.

Clay said, "She is our aunt, our Mama's younger sister."

The mailman waved goodbye as the boys ran up the path to the cabin, yelling for Mama. She hurried out to see what all the excitement was about. They gave her the letter, and a worried look came over her face. She carefully tore the envelope open and began to read. Tears came to her eyes.

She read to the boys that uncle Neal had been injured at work last fall, and had just died in the Bear Creek hospital of pneumonia. She said, "Aunt Olive and your cousin Sally Jane want to move over here to our community so she can be near us. She wants to know if we have room for her to move in. The boys were stunned! They had only met Aunt Olive and Sally Jane once four years ago when they came by to visit. At that time, Sally Jane was six years old, Luke was also six and Clay was eight.

"Mama, we don't have room for them—our cabin is small even for us." said Clay.

"I know, but we can see if the Jones' little cabin is still for sale. It is only a quarter of a mile away."

When Pa came home, they talked. He agreed that they needed to help Aunt Olive and Sally Jane find a home near them. Then Pa went up the road to see the Joneses.

Soon he returned and said the house was not for sale, but it was for rent. That would probably be best for Aunt Olive, anyway. They didn't think she had enough money to buy it.

The next morning Mama wrote her sister with the news. The boys climbed into their tree house and watched down in the valley for the mailman's car to chug up the mountain. When they spied his Nash, they ran to meet him.

When he got to the mailbox, Clay and Luke greeted him and handed him the letter and four pennies for postage. He handed the boys the Sears and Roebuck catalog that Mama had ordered.

They were excited, so after saying goodbye to the mailman, they ran for the cabin. They were anxious to turn to the pages that showed the latest bicycles that Sears had to offer. They had been saving their money and loved to dream about the bike they would choose when they had enough.

As they turned the pages, Mama told the boys that they needed to look at the girl's bikes, too, and to remember that Sally Jane would be here to play with them all summer long.

"WHAT?!" they said in unison. "What do you mean, 'all summer'?! SHE'S A GIRL AND THEY DO GIRL'S STUFF, NOT BOY'S STUFF!!!!! She will probably want to take her doll with her everywhere!"

Mama told them that Sally Jane might surprise them—that she might even be able to outrun them, or climb a tree faster or throw a ball harder.

Clay looked at Luke, and Luke looked back at Clay. Their jaws dropped.

"Does this mean that she has to go everywhere we go and learn ALL OUR PRIVATE SECRETS?" said Clay.

"And what about when we have to take a pee?" asked Luke. Does she have to go with us?" Luke looked very, very disturbed.

Mama laughed out loud and told them they would have to find a bush and go behind it to pee, and when Sally Jane needs to go, she will have to find her own bush.

Luke looked a bit befuddled and said, "Does that mean that we can't still strip all our clothes off and go naked in the pond if she is with us?"

Mama looked a bit startled and said, "Do you boys swim naked in the pond?" They answered that they always did, at least they did before "this girl" shows up.

Clay told Luke that he needed to explain a few things to him about girls, like girls do not stand up to pee, and that they are built different, "so we can't swim naked when she is with us."

Luke just stood there like the cat got his tongue. "AND," Mama said, "you have to let her have her privacy—you cannot go with her around the bush, understand?" Clay said that he was older and would see that everything went okay between "the boys and the new girl."

Mama told the boys they would still have a couple of weeks before Sally Jane arrived.

That night after they climbed the ladder to their bed in the attic, they laid wake for a long time talking about how this girl was going to mess up their boyhood, or maybe ruin their lives forever. Both had a hard time going to sleep that night, but finally Clay heard the panther scream way up the mountain. He thought to himself, "I will tell Sally Jane about the wild panthers and then she will be afraid to ever go into the woods with Luke and me."

He fell asleep with a smile on his face.

Luke was already snoring.

CHAPTER 9

THE RATTLESNAKE AND THE BLACKBERRIES

"Boys, would you go to the edge of the field and pick a quart of blackberries for me? If you do, I will make a blackberry cobbler for supper."

"Sure we will, Mama," the boys said, "We love your cobbler. Can we have buttermilk, too?"

"It's a deal, now get a couple of buckets and get those berries picked!" she teased.

The boys took the buckets and headed up the path to the field where Pa planted a garden each spring. The woods were right behind the field and a bunch of blackberry bushes grew between the field and the woods.

"I'll race you to the blackberries," said Luke. He was two years younger than Clay, and shorter too, but he could give Clay a good race and would sometimes beat him. They started to run and Luke was in the lead until the very last minute when Clay pulled ahead and beat him.

Just as they were getting to the berries, they looked up and saw a hawk circling. Suddenly it dived down to the field near them, then swiftly flapped his wings and rose out of the field with a field mouse in his beak. The mouse squealed for a moment, and then they heard nothing except the flapping of wings.

Clay looked at Luke. "Looks like he has his supper already, but he won't have blackberry cobbler for dessert."

Luke laughed, but then he looked solemn and followed, "But I kind'a feel sorry for the poor little mouse."

"You are right, Luke, but remember what Pa told us: Everything in nature has to have something else in nature to fill its stomach."

"Then what did the little mouse eat for breakfast today—do you know?" glared Luke.

"I think they eat fruit, grain and seeds. Remember the way they get into Pa's grain bin each winter and eat the old cow's food? So, you see, they survive off other things in nature too."

As he was just about finished speaking, he felt something fall on the brim of his cap. He put his hand to his cap and felt something strange. When Clay examined it, he discovered that it was a bone from the poor little mouse that the hawk had devoured while in flight.

"GROSS!" yelled Luke. This was too much for him to take.

They headed into the briar patch to pick berries. Each boy hooked the small buckets onto their belts so they would have both hands free to use for picking. They had also remembered to wear long-sleeved shirts to help protect them from the thorns, and they wore their cowboy boots, as well. This was no time to go barefoot.

"I bet I can pick more berries in half an hour than you can, Clay."

Clay said that he would bet him a bite of his blackberry cobbler that Luke couldn't beat him.

So the picking started. Clay and Luke were each tempted to eat a few berries as they picked, but then the other would have the most berries when the half hour was over.

"Hey, Clay, how do we know when we have picked for half an hour, we don't have a watch."

"I am older and wiser, so I will know when half an hour is over. I will let you know."

They were pushing the tall blackberry bushes aside to get to the berries, when they suddenly heard a rattling noise that they had never heard before. They both immediately knew what the rattling had to be. Both boys froze in their tracks.

They were standing about five feet apart, and right between them was a rattlesnake. Its rattles sounded like BB pellets being shaken in a jar.

Then they spotted the rattler, coiled and ready to strike.

"What do we do?" whispered Luke. His eyes were about to pop out of their sockets!

"Be still and I will try to distract it."

The snake was coiled. He turned his head slowly toward Luke and then back to Clay. When the snake turned again towards Luke, Clay very slowly slipped a green apple out of his pocket. He knew not to make any quick moves. Clay threw the apple into the briars, just in front of the snake.

The sound of the apple startled the snake and it struck towards the briars where Clay threw the apple.

Clay yelled," Run, Luke, for all you are worth!"

Both boys tore through the briars without a thought of the thorns scratching them. Finally, they were back in the open field and Clay stopped running.

"Keep running," yelled Luke, "He may be coming after us!"

"No, we are safe now. The snake felt he was trapped and was warning us not to come closer. If we wanted, we could possibly have slowly backed out and away from him without him striking, but possibly not. At the library, I read a book that said rattlers do not have a lot of venom, so they do not waste it on a strike unless its absolutely necessary."

"You think so, huh," said Luke.

The boys compared the amount of berries in their buckets and they were just about equal.

The discovery of the rattler cut their half an hour of picking time short, so they did not have as many berries for Mama's cobbler, but she said they were correct for leaving the berry patch to the snake.

That night they ate fried potatoes with white gravy poured over them, and fried okra and greens. They told Mama and Pa the whole story about the hawk and the mouse and the rattling noise that scared the wits out of them. While they were waiting for the blackberry cobbler to come out of the oven, Pa got up from the table and left the room. He came back a few minutes later and told Mama that he would get the cobbler and bring it to the table.

Pa had a little rubber rattlesnake that he found one day on the road while walking home. Before bringing in the cobbler, he decided to put the toy snake on top of the cobbler and make everyone laugh.

When he set it on the table and everyone saw it, Luke yelled, Mama screamed and Clay did not know what to do for a minute. Then he realized it was fake and started laughing. Soon the rest realized the joke and were laughing, too.

The family ate the "Rattlesnake Blackberry Cobbler" with a smile on their faces, because the cobbler was delicious and the joke Pa had pulled on the three of them was just perfect.

When the boys climbed up the ladder to their hot, humid room that night they laid on the bed, with nothing over them, not even a sheet.

Clay said, "Well, Luke, looks like we have another chapter for our Tom and Huck book."

Clay looked over, and Luke was already sound asleep. It had been a hard day.

Clay lay awake for a few minutes, then heard the scream of the panther way up in the mountain, and fell asleep.

CHAPTER 10

SALLY JANE AND AUNT OLIVE MOVE TO PANTHER CREEK MOUNTAIN

Both Clay and Luke were snoring and it sounded like a herd of elephants stampeding through the attic.

Mama yelled upstairs: "Wake up, boys! It's a special day! Sally Jane and Aunt Olive arrive with their furniture today! GET UP, you hear me?"

Both boys rolled over in their small bed and looked at each other. This was the day they'd been dreading: The arrival of a girl cousin. They had been told to play with her and share all their adventures.

"Our world is ending today, Luke, things will never be the same…we will always have to go slower when we walk anywhere, or run anywhere, or ride our bike anywhere, because of her! Our life is OVER!"

"And I bet she will be afraid to climb up into our tree house," said Luke.

Mama yelled that they had better get up and eat. They planned to go to the tree house and watch for the truck that would be bringing the newcomers with their furniture.

The boys pulled on their pants, put on clean shirts and climbed down the ladder. Mama had biscuits, white gravy, fried bacon and plum jam on the table waiting for them.

They ate quickly and headed out to the tree house to watch for the truck.

They took a piece of paper and a pencil with them in case they thought of questions they wanted to ask Sally Jane when she arrived. They had no idea what to ask, but they wanted to be ready. Nothing came to their minds.

After a while they saw what looked like a truck way off in the distance kicking up dust on the valley road below. As it got closer, they could tell that it was an old truck with a canvas tarp flapping over the back.

They realized that this had to be it. They were sure because the canvas was covering the furniture.

Then they saw it slowing down to make the turn onto Panther Creek Road.

They hurried down the ladder and ran to the cabin shouting to Mama and Pa that Sally Jane was arriving.

They came running out of the cabin and soon they could hear the old truck struggling to make it up

the mountain. They could hear the trucks gears grinding as the driver had to go into lower gears in order to make it to the top of the hill.

The old truck came to a stop with steam boiling out from under the hood after the long climb. In the truck were the driver, Aunt Olive and a beautiful blonde girl sitting in the front seat between them.

Clay and Luke looked at each other with wide eyes. The little girl they remembered had grown bigger—and beautiful! They had not seen Sally Jane in four years, and both blushed.

Mama and Pa ran to the truck to welcome them, while the boys held back, frozen in their tracks!

Mama told the boys to say hello to Sally Jane and Aunt Olive.

Sally Jane stood beside the truck and gave them a big smile and said, "Hi, y'all!"

Together the boys said, "Hi, Sally Jane, welcome to Panther Creek Mountain."

"Mama says we are going to have a lot of fun playing together." Luke said, "Do you have a doll you take with you everywhere?"

"No, only to bed with me at night." She replied.

"Do you know how to climb a tree?" was all that Clay could think of to say.

"Oh yes, over the mountain where we are moving from, I was one of the best tree climbers in the county. I won a blue ribbon for being the best tree climber at the county fair."

The two boys were speechless.

Finally, Luke said, "Great, then you can come up to our tree house with us. It overlooks the valley far below and is very scary."

"Oh, that sounds great, can I see it tomorrow?"

"Sure, the boys said, tomorrow after breakfast and chores."

Luke, Clay, Mama and Pa helped unload the furniture into the log cabin up the hill that would be Sally Jane's new home, and helped them get settled. Then Mama asked Aunt Olive, Sally Jane and the truck driver to come to their cabin for lunch. Mama sat Sally Jane right between Clay and Luke at the dinner table. Both boys were very quiet.

Finally Clay said, "How old are you, Sally Jane." (He already knew but that was all he could think of to say.)

She said she had just turned nine years old last week.

Clay said he was going to be eleven in a few days and Luke was nine.

"Almost ten!" said Luke.

"Okay, Okay, almost ten," Clay replied. They all laughed.

Sally Jane started asking them a jillion questions and soon the boys found themselves feeling less shy. But they were having trouble getting over how sweet and spirited she was. They had expected something different, but here was a friendly, bright-eyed blonde with a beautiful bouncy ponytail!

After they finished lunch and the truck driver left, they all walked Sally Jane and her Mama back up the trail through the woods to their new cabin and told them goodbye.

Sally Jane threw her arms around each boy, and said, "It is so wonderful having y'all as my sweet cousins! I can't wait to do all the adventures that you two have in mind."

She let go of the boys, and they looked at each other's rosy red faces. Neither of them had ever been hugged by a girl before.

They stammered, "Se-e-e you to-morr-ow, Sal-ly Jane."

The family left and headed down the path to their cabin.

Mama wanted to know what they thought of Sally Jane.

Each waited for the other to speak. Finally Luke said, "Well, she seems smart, and sounds like she is strong and not afraid of anything."

"And pretty, too," Clay chimed in.

Mama told them that they were to remember that she was their first cousin and that they had to protect her and teach her to be safe.

"Yes, like I have to protect Luke," said Clay. Luke thought he could handle himself and did not like Clay's remark, but he let it go.

That night when the boys washed up and climbed the ladder to their attic room, they had already begun to have good feelings about their girl cousin.

"I think we may even learn to like her," said Clay. "What do you think, Luke?"

Luke did not reply—he was already sound asleep. Clay put his head on his pillow wondering if the panther would scream.

Soon it did and he hoped that his new girl cousin had heard it, too.

CHAPTER 11

WHAT ARE WE GOING TO SHARE WITH SALLY JANE?

When the boys awoke the next morning after Sally Jane and her mama arrived, they lay in bed, talking about how many of their secret places they were willing to share with her.

Clay said they could show her the tree house, take her swimming in the pond and take her into the woods to look for squirrels.

"What about our secret cave up in the woods?" said Luke.

"NO, NOT POSSIBLE!" shouted Clay. "No one knows about it except you and me. Remember?"

"Okay, but I was thinking that it might scare her and she might not want to go everywhere with us after that," said Luke.

It was agreed that they would show her the cave someday, but not right away; there were lots of other things to show her first.

Clay and Luke were swinging on the old tire swings that hung from the limbs of the large oak tree near the cabin. This morning they had added a third tire swing for Sally Jane, but she did not yet know about it. They wanted to surprise her.

Sally Jane suddenly appeared wearing overalls, a blue shirt and a bandana. She scared them half to death when she yelled, "You've built me a swing, too! Thank you, thank you!"

As soon as they gathered their wits, they wanted to know if she liked it.

She squealed that she loved it!

Clay wanted to know if she heard the panther screaming in the night because there were a lot of them in the mountain

She said that she was almost asleep when it screamed and that she loved it. She told them that she was excited knowing panthers were in the hills nearby, and hoped to see one someday.

The boys looked at each other in disbelief—they thought she would be scared of panthers!

"Didn't it scare you, Sally Jane?" said Luke.

"No, we had them in the hills near our home over the mountain, too." She said.

The boys looked at each other again, each understanding that this girl had guts and just might make a good playmate after all.

They let her know that there were lots of secret places to show her and that she was in for some real adventures. "We think we are going to like you," Clay said with a red face.

"Thanks," she said, "I already know I like you two."

Both boys blushed.

CHAPTER 12

DON'T GET RUN OVER BY A DEAD CHICKEN

Mama made fried chicken dinners for special occasions, like Easter, Christmas, and sometimes for a special birthday. Today was Clay's birthday.

She made him his favorite cake, pineapple upside-down cake, in her cast-iron skillet.

The family raised a few chickens in order to have eggs to eat. When Mama wanted to make fried chicken for dinner, she had to kill one of them.

So this was a day that was equally frightening and exciting for Clay. Luke had not seen Mama kill a chicken before. He always seemed to be gone with Pa somewhere when it happened. This would be a new experience for him.

Mama got the axe from the barn and tried to catch one of the chickens. Luke and Clay tried to help her. They finally pinned one of the hens into the corner of the fence and caught it.

Mama took it over to a tree stump in the yard. She placed its neck on the stump. Clay told Luke not to watch, but Clay did. After all, he had just turned twelve years old today.

Mama brought down the axe with a thump! The body of the chicken dropped to the ground and then it started to run! This always amazed Clay.

The head was lying on the stump, but the chicken's body did not know it.

For a few seconds it ran in wild circles spraying blood all around the yard. Luke and Clay ran to keep out of its way. They did not want to get blood all over them.

Luke yelled, "Don't let the chicken attack me."

Clay yelled, "Then run faster." Luke did not think that was funny!

They were flabbergasted that something without a head could move so swiftly. "Maybe chickens have their brains in some other part of their body than the head," Luke thought.

Finally, the chicken body fell over and just lay there. The boys stopped running. They were both out of breath.

Mama had a pot of water boiling in a big black kettle over the outdoor fire pit. She dunked the chicken into the hot water. She did this to make it easier to pluck out the feathers. It was very necessary to make sure to have every feather pulled out of the chicken before cooking. Feathers dunked in boiling water did not smell good.

After Mama plucked the chicken, she asked the boys to gather up all the feathers and take them down to throw in the gulley. Luke and Clay gathered them into a large gunnysack and headed down into the field. On the way, they saw a hawk circling overhead. It had already smelled the blood from the chicken and was waiting to see if there might be something for it to eat. All of a sudden, the hawk dived from overhead and came at the boys. Clay flung his hands in the air to scare the hawk away. Luke hit the ground and the hawk made a sharp turn just before striking them. Clay said, "WOW! That was close. That old hawk is trying to scare us. He is seeing how far he can push us. Don't be afraid, Luke, he's just putting on a show."

Luke looked at Clay—he was not so sure about this. Finally the hawk flew away.

Later that day, Mama put a very special meal on the table. She had invited Aunt Olive, Sally Jane, and the Robinsons, "Doc", Bonnie Blue Robinson and Georgie.

Mama put a big platter of fried chicken in the middle of the table, along with mashed potatoes, white gravy, boiled turnip greens, fried okra, salad and her famous buttermilk dinner rolls. The meal looked delicious! Then she put Clay's favorite cake on the table, a pineapple upside-down cake with eleven candles on it. They would be lit later, after everyone finished their meal. Clay could not wait!

When Luke spied the chicken on the platter, he got a funny look on his face. His eyes got big. He suddenly realized that they were about to eat the same chicken that was spurting blood just a little while ago and chasing the boys all around the yard. Clay could see what was coming. Luke was going to tell the whole gruesome story to everyone.

Before Luke could say anything, Clay said, "Luke, tell us the story about falling in the well and how Mrs. Robinson and Georgie helped pull you out." Luke did not want to tell that one. He wanted to tell about the chicken killing, the first one he had ever seen. Mama realized what was happening too. She quickly said, "Let us thank the Lord for the food he has given us."

As she was ready to say the prayer, Luke said, "Don't forget to pray for the poor chicken we had to kill, because I don't think the chicken is very happy with the Lord for giving her to us for our dinner."

Pa, "Doc" and Bonnie Blue all laughed out loud at Luke's request. Sally Jane's ponytail bounced as she laughed.

Mama prayed, then she passed the chicken around the table.

When it came to Luke, he said, "I don't think I would like chicken. But I would like mashed potatoes, white gravy, okra and turnip greens. Oh! And a hot roll with butter"

Then Luke hesitated for a minute and said, "If I don't eat chicken, can I still have some of Clay's delicious birthday cake?"

Mama said, "Yes, Luke." She understood.

After dinner, they all sang "Happy Birthday" to Clay. He made a wish and blew out all eleven candles. They all loved the cake and told Mama how good it tasted. Pa said he had a couple of little gifts for Clay: a Hunting Knife in a scabbard and a whistle that Pa had carved especially for him. Clay smiled and was happy to receive such nice gifts for his birthday.

He went to bed that night hoping his wish would come true. It did. Before he fell to sleep, he heard two panthers screaming. It sounded like they were on two different ridges screaming back and forth.

Clay smiled, and hoped that Sally Jane heard it too, and then he fell asleep.

CHAPTER 13

THE RIVER RAFT AND THE BOOBY TRAP

The Wild Cat River was a slow-moving river that ran through the valley below the ridge where the boys and Sally Jane lived. The boys were excited to point it out to her as they stood by the old tree that hung over the ridge and looked at the beautiful scene below.

Clay told her how good it is to live on this mountain and said there were kids who would give their eyeteeth to live in a place like this and have so many adventures. He said that he and Luke were a lot like Tom Sawyer and Huck Finn. Then he said, "Hey, Sally Jane can be Becky Thatcher!"

Sally Jane agreed to be 'Becky' and said that someone should make a movie about them and show it in the movie house in town.

"That would be the cat's meow," said Luke as he laughed. "What are we going to do today, 'Tom' and 'Becky'?"

Clay thought that they should go down to the river and build a raft like Tom and Huck did and float it in the river, and see how far they could go.

The other two liked the idea.

They realized that if they were going to build a raft, they would have to borrow some of Pa's tools.

They would need an axe, hammer, long nails, rope, and something to use for a paddle and food, of course.

Sally Jane's ponytail bounced up and down as she jumped with excitement. "This is something new for me!" said Sally Jane.

"Us, too," said Luke.

The boys did not sleep well that night; they were so excited about their first big adventure with Sally Jane.

Early the next morning they told Pa what they were going to do and asked if they could borrow some tools.

He just looked at them and smiled. "You don't think we can do it, do you, Pa? Tom and Huck did it and we can do it, too," said Luke.

Pa laughed, not at them, but at the bravery of the boys. He had raised the two boys well and was proud of them and their spirit of exploration.

The boys made peanut butter and jelly sandwiches for the three of them. They put the sandwiches in a cloth bag, then went outside. They hooked an old metal red wagon onto Clay's bike and filled it with tools and food. Then Luke got on his bike and they were off, first to Sally Jane's and then to the river. Sally Jane had stayed up late last night and baked peanut butter cookies for their adventure.

It was further to the Wild Cat River than they had thought, but they finally arrived. Sally Jane suggested that they stop along the way and each eat a cookie to renew their strength.

The boys told her that she made delicious cookies, then smiled at Sally Jane. "Thanks," she said and gave them a big grin.

They searched for a wide place in the river to launch a raft. They hid their bikes, tools and wagon under bushes so no one would discover them while they were on the river.

While they were looking around, they were lucky to find that beavers had been there and had cut down some trees, which would be perfect for the main beams of the raft.

"Why do beavers chew through trees to make them fall and then go off and leave them?" asked Luke.

Clay explained that the beavers did not want the large trunks of the trees but they did need the limbs with the leaves to build dams in the river. In order to get to the limbs, they had to cut down the tree.

"Oh, I get it," said Luke. "That's great for us—we don't have to cut down one tree!"

They took turns swinging the axe for all they were worth. They thought they were going to have to teach Sally Jane how to swing an axe but she said she already knew how, and soon she was cutting as well as the boys. They finally had two six-foot-long logs for beams. The found some old boards that had washed onto the riverbank. They sawed them to the proper lengths and nailed them onto the beams. Before they knew it, they had a genuine "Tom and Huck" raft. They each chose a smaller board for paddles and a long pole to push them from the shore.

Before long, they were floating with the slow-moving current down the peaceful river, just like Huck and Tom. "Sally Jane, how do you like rafting on a river?" asked Luke. "I love it! And I love being with my two cousins and being a part of the adventures," she said and gave each of them a hug. "Yes we make a good team," said Clay. They each ate a sandwich and cookies and drank some sweet tea while their feet hung over the edge into the water. It was heaven.

Clay told them that he heard if you hold some bread in your hand and put your hand under water, along side a raft, you might be able to grab a fish when it comes to nibble the bread, but he went on to say that he guessed one might grab a water moccasin as well.

Luke's eyes got big! Sally Jane's ponytail started bouncing, too.

Suddenly she wanted to know if there were alligators in the river and quickly pulled her feet out of the water.

Clay laughed and said, "No, there are no alligators around these parts." She looked relieved.

Clay tried the bread, and sure enough, a large Bass swam right up and grabbed the bread, but as he did, Clay grabbed the fish and dropped it up on the deck of the raft. It was jumping around and before they could do anything, it jumped back into the river.

"WOW!" said Luke, "Boy, is he going to have a fish tale to tell his wife and baby fish when he gets home!"

They all laughed. "AND, we have a great story to tell Mama, Pa, Aunt Olive and the neighbors up the road," said Clay.

They went a bit further down the river until they spotted a small island in the middle of the river. They had heard kids at school talking about this place.

The kids said that this is where that crazy old man named Ralph Snitsel has the cabin that he claims is his. They said that he won't let anyone go onto the island. He played there when he was a kid, and now that he is old and has taken leave of his senses, he thinks the island is his. He threatens anyone who tries to go there with his shotgun.

They paddled the raft into the bushes along the river and tied it. They wanted to see if they could sneak up and take a look at the old shack.

Luke said, "Well, we might get shot if he is in the shack, so I don't think we should." Sally Jane looked very worried. Clay thought it was okay.

They crawled on their bellies through the bushes so he would not see them if he was in the shack.

All of a sudden they heard the sound of a small motorboat coming up the river. They stopped and listened. It was the first boat they had heard or seen on the river all morning. As they listened, it puttered closer and then they could see through the bushes that it was crazy old Ralph Snitsel. HE WAS COMING TO HIS CABIN, NOT MORE THAN 50 FEET FROM WHERE THEY WERE HIDING!

They froze in place. They were so afraid, they could hardly breathe.

Clay whispered, "We can't make a sound. He is so close that he will hear us, understand, Luke...Sally Jane?"

"Uh-huh," was all they could say, they were so scared. Luke's eyes were ready to pop, and Sally Jane's ponytail did not move.

They watched the old man as he got out of his boat. He had an old ragged hat, and a weathered face with deep lines below his mouth. He started to unload his boat. He had a gunny sack which he placed on the riverbank, then he went back to his boat and got a shotgun!

All three were stunned. Now they could not catch their breath, for sure. It seemed like an eternity before he finally got everything into the cabin.

Then the kids could relax just a little. "What are we going to do?" whispered Luke.

"We have no choice but to wait until he leaves and goes back down river," said Clay.

"But," said Luke. "I have to pee!" "Well, you are going to have to hold it or something, because if you get up, we are all going to be shot!" said Clay.

Despite her fear, Sally Jane giggled nervously.

As they watched the old man, he took some rope and tied it to the door of the shack. They could hear him talk to himself. He said, "I will use this rope and make a booby trap. They will get what they deserve!" he mumbled angrily. "They have always pestered me by breaking into my shack. NO MORE!" I'll tie one end of the rope to door and the other end to the shotgun trigger. When someone tries to break in, they'll pull the door, the gun will go off, and it will blow them away, the little demons!"

Clay, Sally Jane and Luke could not believe their ears. Was he actually going to do this? They watched as he got it all set up. Then he carefully closed the door, with the gun inside, attached to the door. He picked up a long stick and with the end of it, he unlatched the door, and pulled it open. BOOM! Went the shotgun!

The old man let out a sinister laugh. "Now I will just set it back up, leave the shotgun loaded and ready, and go back down the river and wait for it to happen. When it does happen, people will be talking about it. I will silently listen and discover who the little devils were that broke into my shack. Hee, hee, hee," he chuckled with a snaggle-toothed grin, tobacco juice running down the creases of his mouth to his chin.

They watched as he set the booby trap, and then took a minute to appreciate his handiwork before walking back to his little boat, where he climbed in, pulled the rope to start the motor and left.

The three were shocked by what they had witnessed. Now they could breathe!

Clay said, "Now you can pee, Luke."

Luke had been so scared he had forgotten all about peeing.

Clay said, "We have to wait long enough for the old man to be out of range so he won't hear us, then we have to trigger that booby trap, before some other kid comes along and gets killed. We have to take our raft and go down the river to town to tell the sheriff about this horrible thing the old man has done."

So they found the stick that the old man had used and Clay told Luke and Sally Jane to stay back. He carefully poked the door until it started to open and then BOOM! went the shotgun. Clay jumped back and Luke and Sally Jane ran toward the river.

Clay took the shotgun, put it on the raft and they headed downriver with the current taking them towards town.

After about half an hour, they reached town. They pulled up to the riverbank and tied the raft to some bushes. Luke led the way to the street and they headed for the sheriff's office, shotgun in hand.

The sheriff's door was wide open and they walked in, Luke and Sally Jane following Clay. The sheriff gave them a big smile, and then noticed the gun. "What have we here, kids?"

They gave the gun to the sheriff and began to tell their unbelievable story. The sheriff stopped them and yelled to his deputy in the next room to come in so he could hear, too.

As the sheriff listened, he became very concerned. He told them that he was proud that they had the nerve and good sense to discharge the booby trap and come straight to him.

He explained that old Mr. Snitsel was not a bad person, but that he had gotten old and that his mind was doing funny things to him. His wife had died two years ago, leaving him all alone. He said that his neighbors thought he was harmless and they did not want to see him have to go to the state hospital. "But now, it looks like we have a very, very serious situation on our hands."

He asked if they would go with him and his deputy in his boat to the old shack. He wanted them to show him the booby trap setup.

"Sure we will," Clay said. "Do you mind if we tie our raft behind your boat, so we will have it up river again?"

The sheriff agreed. It took a bit longer while pulling the raft, but they were glad they did not have to paddle the raft upriver against the current.

After the sheriff went through the shack and inspected everything, he asked if they wanted him to pull their raft up the river to where their bikes were hidden. They did and thanked him for the offer.

As he let the kids out of the boat, he said, "You're Mac's kids, who live up on the ridge, aren't you?"

Clay said yes and explained that Sally Jane was their cousin.

"He has done a fine job raising you two and I want you to tell him I said so." The sheriff helped the kids get the raft tied to the bushes on the riverbank before leaving.

"Now I have to go get the old man and take him to the state hospital for his safety and everyone else's. You three have done absolutely the right thing by telling me about this. The county thanks you for your bravery. You may have saved some other person's life."

"We are happy to have helped," said Clay.

They waved goodbye as the sheriff motored away down the river.

"I will tell you one thing," said Clay, "This story would be a good one to tell if we ever write a book like Tom and Huck and Becky."

They got their bikes, tools and wagon out of the bushes and headed up the hill toward their little cabins on the ridge.

Sally Jane waved good-bye to the boys as she headed further on up the hill. She was not sure if she should tell her Mama about this day's adventure. She did not want her Mama to worry, or to stop her from having more exciting adventures with her cousins.

The boys had a wild story to tell Mama and Pa tonight at supper, as they enjoyed potato soup, fried okra, corn bread, buttermilk and a big piece of blueberry pie.

CHAPTER 14
THE TRAIN SCARE

One day, the boys decided to ride their bikes up to Sally Jane's cabin and get her to go with them into town to do some exploring.

Sally Jane wanted to know what they were going to explore.

Clay told them that he was lying awake during the night and heard the old freight train slowly work its way over the tracks that wind through Wild River Valley. It blew its horn at each road crossing and it fascinated him and got him thinking about trains. He thought that they should ride the bikes down into town and go to the train yard and watch the men working on the trains.

Sally Jane and Luke thought that was a good idea, one that they had not done before.

On the way, they went into Mr. Hollins' gas station and had a Pepsi, then headed down the road that ran through the valley and into town. They passed by the courthouse, Mr. Dangle's Shoe Store, Crow's Soda Fountain, and the movie theater, then went down the long hill at full speed towards the railroad tracks and the train yard.

As they rode through the train yard gate, they noticed a sign that said, NO TRESPASSING!

Sally Jane stopped her bike and said, "We will get into trouble if we go in there—let's leave."

Clay said, "I don't think it means the three of us can't go in."

Luke said, "Then who do you think they DO mean?"

"Just act like we know what we are doing and I'm sure everything will be fine," Clay said.

The men were hooking and unhooking the huge freight cars and did not see the kids enter the yard. They got off their bikes and walked out onto a small

train bridge so the could watch the men working. There were handrails on the side of the bridge.

The bridge was about fifty feet long and went over a small creek. They walked to the middle of the bridge. All of a sudden, a big engine and cars started moving toward them. They pressed their bodies against the handrails as the train started getting closer. They grabbed the handrails and held on.

It was only then that the men saw the kids. The engineer started blowing his whistle and waving for them to get off the bridge. Clay, Luke and Sally Jane could feel the suction from the train starting to pull them towards it. But it was too late to run off the bridge. The train was starting to move fast. They had no idea of the great amount of suction the train would create as it picked up speed. The sound was deafening.

Clay yelled to Luke and Sally Jane, " Hold on and pray!"

Luke started yelling, "Lord, don't let us get sucked under this train!"

Sally started crying and screaming. They held onto the handrail with all their strength until the engine and eight freight cars were finally past.

Clay looked at Luke and Sally Jane. They were both covered with soot that came from under the train.

Luke finally tried to smile, while Sally Jane was trying to wipe the tears as they streamed through the black soot on her face. Luke also had tears in his eyes.

"Boy, am I glad to see those white teeth, Luke," Clay said, "and you prayed good."

Luke smiled again, he believed in prayer more than Clay did and Clay believed in Luke.

"I thought for a few seconds there that we were going to be killed," said Clay. He had tears in his eyes, too. Sally Jane was too stunned to say anything.

On the way home, they stopped at a sandy shoreline of the Wild Cat River. All three stripped off their clothes down to their underwear, waded into the water and tried to wash the soot from their faces and arms. They did not want their mamas to know where the soot came from or how close they had come to being killed.

This had been a dangerous new adventure for the boys and their cousin and one they would not forget anytime soon. They made a pact between themselves that they were not going to tell anyone about how foolish they had been, including their best friend, Georgie Robinson.

When they got to the boy's cabin, Sally Jane waved goodbye and headed up the road to her cabin. Her Mama told her the boys would probably do some crazy things, so for her to be careful. Today, she learned that her Mama was right.

CHAPTER 15

SALLY JANE'S JACKKNIFE

The morning chores were finished and Clay and Luke were thinking about what they should do next. It was a cooler day, with clouds covering the sky, but it did not look much like rain.

Clay and Luke each had a jackknife, but Sally Jane did not. They thought she needed one, too so they decided to get Sally Jane and ride their bikes down into town. They would get her one at the Army surplus store.

This would be great because then they would all have the same tools for scouting the woods and ravines. They decided that they would buy it for her as a gift.

They would take a gunny sack with them to pick up cold drink bottles along the road to town and sell them at Hollins' store. A lot of people drank cold drinks as they drove and just threw the empty bottles out the car windows. They were wasting their money as far as the boys were concerned and were littering the roadway too. But the money the people threw away was theirs to get and would help them buy Sally Jane's knife.

They went to Sally Jane's cabin to tell her the news and when they did, she jumped up and down and her ponytail jumped up and down with her.

They asked Aunt Olive if Sally Jane could ride her bike into town with them. She agreed, and Sally Jane was very excited. The boys were happy to do something special for her.

Sally Jane squealed, "I have always wanted a jackknife of my very own and now my sweet cousins are going to get me one!"

Aunt Olive asked the kids if they needed to take lunch with them for the trip. They thought that was a good idea, because they would be gone most of the day.

Aunt Olive looked at the sky and saw that it was clouding up and thought it might rain. She wanted to know what they would do if it started to pour and there was lightning?

"We have survived rain storms and lightning before, so we will figure something out," Clay bragged.

She let Clay know that she depended on him to use his good judgment in case of a big storm. This made Clay feel grown up and he was proud to hear her say this because it showed that she trusted him.

Aunt Olive made plum jelly and peanut butter sandwiches and put them in a cloth sack along with some fresh cookies. They thanked her and rode off on their bikes.

They flew down Mountain Creek Road, stirring up dust as they went. Wild River Road was paved and made bike riding smoother and more fun. There was very little traffic on the road today, so it made it easier to watch for cold drink bottles. They could ride on both sides of the road without being as concerned about the danger of cars.

As they saw bottles in the ditches, they stopped, picked them up and put them into the gunnysack that Clay had tied to the handlebars of his bike. In the two miles they rode into town, they collected 26 bottles.

They stopped at Hollins' store to sell the bottles and collected fifty-two cents. Now the two boys would each need to contribute only forty-eight cents between them.

Sally Jane had never been to an Army surplus store before. Her eyes grew wide and bright as she looked at the piles and piles of stuff in the huge store.

The boys showed her their favorite places in the store, the knives, the camping gear and the fishing gear. Sally Jane asked where all this stuff came from.

"We get it from the army," said a booming voice behind them. It was Mr. Jones, the store manager.

"The army has a lot of things they do not need anymore when a war is over, so they sell it to stores like mine."

Sally Jane's eyes twinkled when the boys told her to pick out the knife she liked best. All knives were one dollar each, just as the boys remembered.

They wandered around the store for about an hour and then they thought they had better find a tree to sit under and eat their lunch. As they sat down, they could hear thunder rolling through the sky away off in the distance. The clouds were getting thicker and it was getting darker, even though it was early afternoon.

"I think we were wrong about it raining today," said Luke. "It looks like we had better get on our bikes and ride like crazy. We need to get home before it starts raining and lightning!"

They all agreed that their day in town was suddenly over. They got on their bikes and peddled as fast as they could down Wild River Road. The skies darkened quickly and then there was a big bolt of lightning that struck close by, followed by deafening thunder. Startled, they looked at each other without saying a word. Clay was quickly rethinking what he had told Aunt Olive about not fearing thunderstorms, and his expression of concern frightened Luke. Sally Jane was silent.

The wind started to blow and soon they felt rain hitting their faces. At first it was not hard rain, but then another bolt of lightning hit even closer to them, followed by another huge boom. The rain became harder. It was beginning to be difficult to ride against the wind and rain.

Clay yelled, "There might be a tornado coming! There is a bridge right up the road— let's head for it." The other two said nothing and silently followed Clay's lead as he dropped his bike beside the road and ran down the bank and under the bridge.

Soon they were under the bridge looking out. It started to really rain hard; sheets of water fell from the sky. They watched small trees bend over in the fierce wind. Then they heard a noise like a train rumbling over the bridge, and suddenly they feared that it was a tornado! After all, they'd often heard people talk about tornados sounding like freight trains when they touched down from the sky.

Clay shouted, "Lay down flat on the ground and hold on to the bushes!"

As the wind picked up force where they lay, they held on to the bushes for dear life. It seemed like forever, but finally the wind and the horrible noise stopped and there was silence.

They all looked at each other. They were shocked by what had just taken place. "Are you two alright?" said Clay. In trembling voices they each responded, "Yes."

They sat there for a few minutes and tried to calm down. All of a sudden, Luke looked up the ditch and saw water gushing down toward them from the cloudburst of rain just a few minutes before. "Run!" he yelled. "Flash flood!" They jumped up and ran up the bank to higher ground. In a flash, the ditch filled with water.

"We would probably have all drowned if you had not been alert, Luke," said Sally Jane. Luke teared up a bit at her words. She made him feel like a hero, but he did not want the others to know because it made him feel shy.

"Luke, You are our hero!" Clay shouted. Now Luke burst into tears. Sally Jane did too. They were so relieved to know they had just survived a terrible situation. Clay did not cry, but he understood their feelings.

As they looked around, they saw that the tornado had torn the roof off a nearby barn and had pulled trees out of the ground. Luckily, they did not see any homes destroyed along the road.

When they started to ride home, they wondered if Mama, Pa and Aunt Olive were okay. They were concerned.

They topped the hill near their cabins, and saw some broken trees, but the cabins looked like they had not been damaged.

Pa, Mama and Aunt Olive were all on the porch anxiously watching for the kids and ran out to meet them as soon as they came into view. All of them were glad to see that no one was hurt.

Pa was the first to speak. "We were worried to death about you kids. Did the tornado hit the ground where you were?"

In unison, they all began to excitedly talk at once. "Wait, only one of you speak at a time!" said Mama. "I want to hear every detail."

Each one told their version of the hair-raising experience.

Then Sally Jane said, "I want to tell how brave Clay was during the storm. He led us to safety under the bridge, and then Luke spied the flash flood coming at us while we were still under the bridge. He saved us. I am so proud of my smart, sweet cousins!" and she gave them huge hugs.

Then she showed everyone her new jack knife. "Now we are equal when we go into the woods together," she beamed.

When they went to bed that night, Sally Jane carved in the rafters above her bed in the attic, "I love my cousins." Then she closed her knife, put it under her pillow and went to sleep with a smile on her face.

The boys lay in their bed and talked for a long time about their exciting but scary day. Luke said, "You know, Clay, We are really lucky that Sally Jane moved here. She is very special."

"I agree," said Clay. "Today we found out that she can survive any adventure with us. Yes, she *is* special."

He looked over at Luke, but he was already sound asleep. Then Clay heard a scream. He was glad to know that the panther had survived the storm as well.

CHAPTER 16

SELLING HOT DOGS AT THE OLD SWIMMING HOLE

One day Mama brought some wieners and buns home from Mr. Stewart's grocery store. Clay and Luke asked if they could build a fire in the fire pit behind the cabin and roast the wieners instead of cooking them in the kitchen.

They told her it would be like camping out in the woods.

Mama said that was a good idea, and for one of them to run up the road and invite Sally Jane and Aunt Olive to join them for the roast. Luke jumped on his bike and headed to Sally Jane's cabin. Clay got a fire started and Mama brought out the mustard, buns and sweet ice tea.

Soon, Sally Jane, and Aunt Olive joined them. Using their pocketknives, the kids whittled the ends of small branches to points so the wieners would slide on easily for roasting. They had a blast roasting the wieners just like they were camping out.

As they were sitting around the fire, they watched the fireflies in the dark woods. All of a sudden, Clay had an idea. "Mama, if you will buy some extra wieners and buns next week, Luke, Sally Jane and I can take them to the swimming hole on Sunday afternoon and sell hot dogs to the people who are swimming. There are a lot of families who go there each Sunday."

Pa said the families probably brought their own sandwiches, so they might not be able to sell them.

Mama thought that the idea had some merit, so she suggested that next Sunday the boys and Sally Jane take only six wieners, six buns, mustard and ketchup and sweet tea to see if they would sell.

When Sunday arrived, Mama put the hot dog makings in a sack. The boys put on their swimming suits, hopped on their bikes, stopped for Sally Jane and they all headed for the swimming hole under the large old steel bridge on Wild Cat River.

Several families were already there when the boys and Sally Jane arrived. Clay told Luke and Sally to gather up dry sticks and old broken tree limbs. They built a fire and had it raging within a few minutes. The fire caught everyone's attention and soon the people started to gather around wanting to know what the kids were doing.

Clay said. "Well when the fire dies down a bit, we are going to use an old family recipe and roast some wieners like you have never tasted before."

Luke looked at Clay in amazement, wondering what he was talking about, but Luke kept his mouth shut. Sally Jane just stood by and grinned. She admired how Clay took charge of things.

Clay took a wiener out of the sack and poured some of Mama's sweet tea over it, but he did not tell the people that it was tea. He just said it was the secret family formula. He put the wiener over the fire and soon the wiener was roasted. Luke put on mustard and Sally Jane added ketchup on the buns and Clay laid on the wiener.

Then Clay said, "We want each one of you to take a bite and tell us if you have ever tasted such a delicious hot dog."

They passed around the hot dog and everyone took a bite.

"Best dad-gum hot dog I ever had," said one of the men. The others pitched in saying that the special family recipe was just great. They asked if they could buy some of the dogs from the boys.

"We only have five left today, but next Sunday we will have many more, so tell all your friends. And they are only 15 cents each."

So the next Sunday afternoon they had the fire going and set up a temporary table made from a couple of boards. They made a hand-painted sign that said:

Luke and Clay's Famous Family Recipe Hot Dogs
Sally Jane's Famous Sweet Tea.

Before long, more families arrived and lined up to try the secret family Hot Dog recipe. Some people thought it had the taste of honeysuckle, some thought it tasted like sassafras, and one man even said it tasted a bit like sweet tea. When the man said that, Luke and Sally Jane quickly looked over at Clay to see how he would react.

Clay stayed calm and said, "Well, I would not say anyone is wrong. It is just good to hear that everyone thinks the Hot Dogs are delicious and made even better when eaten with Sally Jane's sweet tea. Sally

Jane turned red, then let out one of her great big grins.

For the rest of the summer, every Sunday afternoon Clay, Luke and Sally Jane took hot dogs, sweet tea and small jars of 'Mama's Wild Plum Jam' and jars of 'Aunt Olive's Sweet Pickles' to sell. They did well enough with the sales that the three them would have almost enough money to buy new bikes next Christmas.

Even better, they were proud to know they could make money from almost nothing.

CHAPTER 17

RACCOON HUNTING AT NIGHT

Ol' Larry Tuffy was a coon hunter who lived about half a mile up Panther Creek Road from the boy's cabin. He used the backside of his cabin to dry the hides from raccoons he had shot. He nailed them to the cabin logs after he stripped the skins from the bodies of the coons.

His work always fascinated the boys. They thought that the hides might have a bad smell, but there was hardly any smell to them at all.

One time before Sally Jane moved to the ridge, Ol' Larry gave two hides to the boys. Mama cut them and made each of the boys a Coon Skin Cap. They were so proud to wear them, they felt like Davy Crockett.

When Sally Jane first arrived, she asked the boys where they got those neat caps. They explained where the caps came from and told her that one day they would take her up to Ol' Larry's cabin and introduce her. They hoped he would offer her a coonskin, too.

One morning Clay and Luke thought they heard Ol' Larry chopping wood up at his cabin. They rushed up to Sally Jane's cabin. "Sally Jane! Today is the day to meet Larry." She was excited.

The boys put on their coonskin caps and the three kids rode their bikes to Ol'Larry's cabin.

As they rode into Ol' Larry's yard, the old coonhounds came from behind the cabin to meet them with a friendly bark and wagging tails. The boys kneeled down and rubbed the dog's long ears. Sally Jane watched and did the same. The dogs seemed to like Sally Jane immediately.

Ol' Larry stopped chopping wood and came around the cabin to meet them. The boys introduced Sally Jane and said. "This is our cousin and she can do anything in the woods that we can do." "Well, said Ol' Larry, "I guess if she's gonna do what ye boys do, then she needs one of them there coon caps too. What do ye think, Sally Jane?"

Sally Jane grinned from ear to ear. "Yes, sir, I would love to have one!"

"Then we gonna go round the cabin and pick one for ye" he said. When they reached the back of the cabin, Sally Jane could not believe her eyes! One coonskin after the other covered the wall of the cabin. "You look at this here wall and choose the one ye like best."

Sally Jane looked and didn't know how to choose —they all looked alike to her. But she knew he wanted her to choose, so she pointed to one. Ol'

Larry said, "Well, my girl, that one ain't done drying yet, so you need'a pick 'nother one."

She did and this time he smiled. "That's the best of the bunch." He took his hammer, pulled out the nails and handed it to her. Her eyes beamed. She was going to have her very own Davy Crockett cap too.

"Oh, thank you, thank you!" she said and ran over to give him a hug. He blushed the color of a ripe tomato. "Ye welcome," he said.

"Now, kids, I have a question," he continued. "Would you three like'a go coon hunting with me and my hounds one night this week?"

Their eyes all got big as wagon wheels. "Yes, SIR!" they said together. "When?"

"Well, tomorrow night when there's suspos'a be a full moon, and that's good fer huntin' coons. How 'bout that?"

"Great, what time? Do we need a gun?" said Clay.

"No, I do the shootin' and you do the watchin' and the hounds will find' em and lead us to the tree they chase 'em into. See ya here at dark."

They thanked Ol' Larry and rode down the hill toward home as fast as the wind.

The next night, they arrived at Ol' Larry's a little before dark. The hounds already sensed what was going to happen and they were howling out a chorus.

Ol' Larry had his rifle and a flashlight ready. He was as excited as the coonhounds.

Larry led the way for the three kids, but the hounds had already run far ahead. The dogs were silent at first, then they started to howl for all they were worth. Ol' Larry ran. They's already got one of 'em uppa tree," he yelled. "Come on."

The kids ran after him, through briars and branches, trying to keep up with him. He finally stopped under a big oak tree. He shined his flashlight high up into the branches and they saw bright eyes

looking back at them. But there were six eyes looking back, not two like they expected. They realized that four of the eyes were baby raccoons'. They were on their Mama's back, holding on for dear life.

Suddenly, everything changed. Sally Jane said, "Please, Mr. Larry, don't shoot the mama, what will her babies do?" Luke jumped in and said that he agreed with Sally Jane.

Ol' Larry looked at Clay, then up in the tree and raised his riffle. "Wait, said Clay, "I agree with them. We should not shoot the Mama."

Ol' Larry gave them all a look of disbelief. "How am I gonna 'splain this to my dogs? All they knows is to hunt."

Ol' Larry lowered his gun and said, "Let's head home. Come on, dogs." The dogs looked bewildered, let out a few more yelps, then ran ahead toward home.

As they were ready to leave Ol' Larry's cabin, the kids told Larry that they felt they had spoiled his evening, but he told them that they were right. You should not shoot a Mama coon.

When they got home they told their parents what took place. The parents were pleased that the kids had stood up for what was right.

Clay said, "I bet that Ol' Larry will think we are all sissies." Pa spoke up and said, "No, I suspect that Larry will respect you for what you did."

"I hope so," said Clay.

It had been a long day. Luke finally fell asleep. He dreamed of a bunch of little raccoons that lost their Mama. He was relieved the next morning to wake up and realize it was only a dream.

Clay lay awake thinking about the whole ordeal, and what he would have done if Larry had pulled the trigger and killed the Mama raccoon. Then he thought: *Luke, Sally Jane and I would have had to bring the babies to the cabin and raise them.* Then he heard the panther scream; he rolled over and fell asleep.

CHAPTER 18

PA BRINGS HOME A SURPRISE

One day "Doc's" truck pulled up to the cabin and Pa got out carrying something. Clay and Luke ran out to meet him.

He said, "Go get Mama. I have a big surprise. He had a cardboard box in his arms and it appeared quite heavy. Clay and Luke wondered what it could be.

Mama came out to the porch. Pa smiled and opened the box. It was a beautiful radio in a wooden case. It had a big battery that was larger than the radio.

Pa said, "We have waited a long time to have a radio in our home. I have been hoping that the electric company would soon run its power line up the ridge, so we could have modern conveniences. But they don't seem to think there are enough people living on the ridge to make it worth it to run the lines up here. So the only way we can have a radio is to run it off battery power. That's why I have been saving money to buy a radio and a battery."

They were all amazed. It was a beautiful wooden one, nicer than any of the other furniture in the cabin. "When can we listen to it?" they all said at once.

Pa said he would get it set up in the afternoon and everyone could listen to it in the evening. He said he had to run a wire antenna from the cabin to a nearby tree in order to get better reception. He told everyone go on with what they were doing and at about 6:00, there would be a "family radio hour."

The boys said they had to tell Sally Jane the news, and they ran, shouting before they actually got to her cabin. Sally Jane came running out of the cabin thinking that something terrible had happened.

The boys were breathless. "We—we just—got—a-a-brand—new Radio!" they blurted out.

"You got what?" cried Sally Jane…. "A real radio?"

"Yes! Can you believe it?' They were both trying to tell the news at once. When they calmed down a bit, they told her the whole story and said that she and her mama were invited to hear the first show on the new radio and to come for supper. too.

"We will all eat supper and listen to music at the same time!" said Clay with a grin. They had all listened to radios before down in town where people had electricity, but this was a first for the ridge. "We will be the only folks on the ridge with a radio in their home," boasted Luke.

By evening Pa had the antenna strung from a tree up to the cabin. He attached the radio to the battery and soon he had everything ready to go.

Everyone sat quietly while Pa attempted to tune in the first station. The radio hummed, squawked and squeaked a few times, and then they heard the voice of a man reporting the weather forecast for the mountain area. He said it was going to continue to be warm, but showers were forecast for the next several days.

Clay spoke up, "If we had had this radio last week, we could have heard the weather forecast and would have known that a storm was coming toward our area before we rode our bikes to town. It could have saved us from the danger we went through under the bridge."

They all agreed with Clay.

Next was a country music show from Nashville. The family all loved hearing songs by Hank Williams, Hank Snow, Ernest Tubb, and Gene Autry. They sang along with the music, although they didn't know most of the words.

A detective story was next. It was filled with suspense that caused the kids to huddle close to each other. Everyone loved it.

They listened for another hour, then Mama said, "It has been an exciting evening, but we all need to go to bed."

Sally Jane and her Mama thanked them for a fun evening and headed up the trail to their cabin. Clay and Luke offered to walk them home.

When they returned, they asked Pa if he would leave the radio going for a little while after they went to bed. They wanted to hear a little more music before they fell asleep.

He told them he would leave it on for another fifteen minutes.

The boys climbed the ladder and listened to more country music coming from the new radio below, and then drifted off to sleep.

The panther screamed, but neither heard it.

CHAPTER 19

SATURDAY AFTERNOON BATHS

One day, Luke, Sally Jane and Clay sat in the tree house looking out across the valley below. They were trying to come up with new ideas for making money.

"We have to figure out something that the people in our little community want and will pay money to get," said Clay, "but what is it that they really need and don't have?"

Sally Jane responded, "Well, it seems to me that a lot of these mountain people need a good hot bath!"

Both boys looked at her and burst out laughing. "No I am serious," she insisted, "Everyone up on the ridge takes their Saturday night baths in a little old galvanized tub like we do, and it's just not enough! None of us have running water or indoor bathrooms. We only have outdoor toilets. It would be wonderful to take a hot bath in a big tub!"

This time the boys looked seriously at her and did not laugh. They understood that she meant business.

"What do you think we should do, Sally Jane, go cabin to cabin and wash the people down?" Luke wisecracked. Clay laughed. Sally Jane did not.

"Enough of your smart remarks, Luke. We have got to think of a plan."

They stretched out on their backs in the tree house and thought about how to their make their idea work.

Clay had an idea and said, "Okay, I have a thought brewing, let me just think a bit longer. Okay, I think I got it! Listen and see what you think. Pa has been doing some plumbing work for old Mr. Snoots at his Tourist Courts down in town They are remodeling some of the bathrooms and replacing the cast-iron bathtubs with new, modern ones. Mr. Snoots told Pa that he could have the old tubs if he would carry them away."

"So what are you saying," quipped Luke, "is haul the old tubs cabin to cabin, draw water from their well and give each family a bath!"

"Stop being a wise guy, Luke," said Sally Jane, "Let's hear what Clay is thinking."

So Clay started to explain, "We will ask Pa to bring home two of the old tubs. We have the old back shed that we can divide into two small rooms; one tub in each room. We already have gravity flowing water to Mama's kitchen from the spring up on the hill behind the cabin. We can run another pipe down the hill to our bathtubs and have the neighbors come on Saturdays and pay us to take a bath in a large tub!"

"But the water will be freezing cold," said Sally Jane. "How can we heat the water?"

"I know," beamed Luke. "Remember last year Pa brought an old hot water heater home that you have to build a fire underneath in order to heat the water in the tank. We will ask him to let us use it and we will be in business."

So the plans started to take shape. "Let's make a list," said Sally Jane. She ran to her cabin and brought back paper and a pencil and they made a list of things to do:

Build divider in shed to make two rooms.

Ask Pa to bring the tubs up the mountain.

Place old hot water heater outside near the shed.

Run old hose from the water spring to the hot water heater.

Gather branches and cut wood to burn under the hot water heater.

Decide how to advertise the new, wonderful thing available for our little community.

It was getting late in the afternoon when they heard Mama call out, "Come to supper! And that means you too, Sally Jane. Go get your Mama and tell her to join us."

Soon they were all sitting down to a steaming bowl of Mama's potato soup, hot cornbread, wild possum grape jam and a glass of buttermilk.

"We have exciting news to tell you," said Clay with a big smile on his face. Both Luke and Sally Jane, with her ponytail jumping were squirming with excitement in anticipation of their parents' reaction.

Clay told them the whole idea from start to finish. All three parents sat at the table, stunned.

Finally Mama spoke, "Do you think people will leave their own cabins and come here to take a Saturday bath? What about privacy? Do they bring clean underclothes with them? Do they bring their own towels and soap, and who helps the old people in and out of the tub? I think you three have a lot more questions to answer before you start."

Sally Jane's Mama spoke up and said, "Well, I think they might have something here. Let's see if we can work out the details."

"Okay," said Pa, "but I ain't gonna be the one to help the old men in and out of the tub, or the old ladies. either!" They all laughed.

The next week came and Pa brought the tubs home in "Doc" Robinson's old truck, the kids hooked up the pipe from the water spring and built a wooden wall down the middle of the shed room. Pa helped set up the old hot water heater behind the shed and the kids used some old large pine boards to make a sign. The sign was nailed to the tree by the road and it said:

> *Clay, Luke and Sally Jane's*
>
> *Hot Saturday Family Baths in a Real Bathtub,*
>
> *Reserve your space now!*
>
> *One tub of hot water, 50 cents, can be used for one or more family members.*
>
> *Time limit 30 minutes per tub*
>
> *Bring your own towels and soap*
>
> *Open from 1:00 till 5:00 Saturdays*

In addition to making the sign, they went from cabin to cabin on Panther Creek Ridge and told the neighbors. Some looked shocked when they were told of the new business, but Clay, Luke and Sally Jane soon had them relaxed as they explained the privacy and how more than one family member could use the same hot water, which would make it more affordable for some of more meager means.

Clay suggested that they should all try the hot bath idea out on the family members before they opened to the public. Luke and Sally agreed. They told Pa and Mama and Aunt Olive the plan.

"Tomorrow is Friday, so let's all have a hot bath! If there are kinks, we will have time to work them out before our opening on Saturday," said Clay.

Luke and Clay woke up early and went out to start the wood fire burning under the hot water tank. Sally Jane smelled the smoke from her cabin and knew what they were doing, so she came running down the hill to help.

Soon the parents appeared with soap and towels, grinning from ear to ear. The kids ran the hot water in each of the tubs. Sally Jane went with her Mama to the women's tub. Mama said she would take her bath after Aunt Olive was finished. The boys settled Pa into his tub. Pa burst out singing an old mountain

song, "One Bath a Week Is all You Need!"

Mama could hear him singing from outside the shed. Aunt Olive and Sally Jane could hear too, so everyone joined in singing, splashing and laughing.

The kids went outside and put more wood on the fire so the rest could have a clean tub of hot water for their baths.

Pa, Mama and Aunt Olive looked fresh as daisies after their baths. They were very happy, feeling really clean.

The tubs were filled with fresh hot water. It was time for Luke, Sally Jane and Clay to have their turn. Sally Jane went into the women's room, giggling as she went. They could hear her through the wall, saying, "Oh, the water is hot and wonderful and the tub is so big!" The boys were giggling too. "We can hear you, Sally Jane! It sounds like you are having fun!" She squealed back as she splashed about. "I Love it!!! Are you in your tub yet?"

Clay yelled, "Luke is in the tub and is holding his breath underwater. This is great!" "Hurry, Luke so I can have my bath!" said Clay.

Later, the kids dried and put on fresh clothes. Everyone had huge smiles.

The trial run was a success! The whole family was clean and happy. None of them had been in a big bathtub before so this was a special adventure!

The next day was Saturday, the sign was up, and although no one had reserved a time spot, the kids built a fire under the hot water heater. Soon they could hear the water boiling in the tank, but no one came by for a bath.

Finally they heard a horse and wagon come down the road carrying old Mr. and Mrs. Smithson who lived about a mile away. "We hear ye got hot water baths just like in town," said Mr. Smithson, "is that right?"

"Yes we do," said the three in unison, "and you are our first guests!"

"If ye say we are the first, don't ye think one of us should have a free bath?"

All three said, "Of course, our first customer should have a free bath! In fact you can each have a tub and it will only cost you a total of 50 cents."

As they helped the old couple out of the wagon, Mrs. Smithson told them that they brought new towels that she had made out of cloth feed bags, and a batch of new lye soap made just for the occasion.

Sally Jane took Mrs. Smithson to the "women's bath" and the boys helped Mr. Smithson to his. He said, "Ye boys probably don't know, but the Mrs. and me has never been in one of these here long tubs before, and I am ready to jump in!"

Each of the Smithsons settled into their tubs with big grins on their faces. When the thirty minutes bath time was up, the alarm clock went off.

As they climbed into their wagon to go home, they told the three kids how happy they were and how clean they felt. The old man reached under the seat of the wagon and brought out a pint jar of honey from his beehives and said, "This here is for your Mama, and tell her that I said that you are all dad-gum good kids."

"Thank you!" they said and waved as the Smithson's wagon pulled away. Suddenly the wagon stopped and old Mr. Smithson yelled back, "We are gonna stop at every cabin we pass and tell them people that they ought'a get down here and get a bath!"

Within an hour, other families started to arrive to try out the new baths. Some wanted a single bath for each, while two families wanted the whole family to use the same water to save money.

Clay, Sally Jane and Luke made $3.00 for the afternoon's work and were thrilled.

After that first Saturday, the neighbors reserved time for their baths and the business venture did very well through the summer until fall.

When fall arrived, a new sign was nailed to the tree by the road that read:

> *"Hot Baths closed for the winter, see you in the spring"*

CHAPTER 20

THE MOUNTAIN PEDDLER

"Look! What is that coming up the trail?" exclaimed Sally Jane, lying on her belly and looking over the edge of the tree house floor. Both boys jumped up to see what she was talking about. They all squinted against the afternoon sun, and made out the form of an old bent man struggling up the mountain on foot.

They looked hard and saw what they suspected to be an old peddler because he had a huge pack on his back.

"Mama and Pa have told us that peddlers used to come through these parts before Luke and I were born. They said that sometimes they would ask to spend the night in exchange for some of the goods they sold. Let's run down the road to meet him and see what he is selling."

As they approached the old man, they could see that he had ragged clothes and no shoes. He looked very old with deep furrows in his face. He was having a difficult time on the steep trail and he did not see the three approaching him until they were right in front of him. They could see that he had he did not have good eyesight. His eyes looked cloudy.

"Hello friend," said Clay, "Welcome to Panther Ridge." The old man was startled at first because he had not seen the kids, but now broke into a big toothless grin and said, "How nice of you to call me friend. Do you kids know me from when I traveled these parts before?" But then, he realized they were too young to have known him. He had not been on this ridge for 15 years, when he was a much younger man.

"No, we have not met you before, but you have probably met our Mama and Pa," said Luke. "They have lived on this ridge since they were both young. I am Luke and this is my brother Clay and the pretty one is our cousin, Sally Jane." Sally Jane blushed.

The old peddler said his name was Oscar. They all said hi and shook his hand.

The old man asked them if their Mama was home. He said he had some pots and pans that she might like. The boys said, no, that she was at work in town. He then asked if their Pa was home and again they said no. Sally Jane said, "My Mama is home and I am sure she would like to see the things you have for sale."

As they walked past Clay and Luke's cabin, the old peddler said, "I remember this cabin from years back when I used to peddle these parts. I don't know if your parents lived here or not."

Then he asked if he might have a drink of water, or if they had a water spring nearby.

They told him they would be happy to get him a glass of water from their cabin. Luke ran to get it and when he returned, he found the peddler sitting on the edge of the porch taking things out of the bag that he carried on his back.

First he took out some pots and pans that were bright and shiny. Sally Jane, Clay and Luke's eyes lit up when they saw them because they knew their mamas would love to own them. Then he reached deeper into the bag and they could hear sounds of tin objects rubbing together. He pulled out two little metal cars and a small rubber doll. The kids' eyes lit up once again. Sally Jane knew that he meant for the doll to be for her, but she really wanted a toy car, too.

"Do you have any more little cars in your bag, sir?" she said. He looked quizzically at her, then said, "Yes I do have another one," and pulled out another car. She handed the doll back to him. "How much do the cars cost?" asked Clay.

He told them that the cars were 25 cents each, but he wanted to show them something about the cars that a lot of people didn't know. He took one of the painted tin cars and showed them that in very small letters, it said Made in Japan on the trunk lid, then he turned it over and told the kids to look through the window openings to the inside roof of the cars, "What do you see?" he asked.

They all looked and said, "We see the word 'Prince Albert; printed inside. Why? What does that mean?" Then they looked at the other two cars, and found words or pictures printed inside each of them.

The old peddler said, "Sit on the porch beside me and I will explain it to you. As you all know, the World War II ended several years ago. Japan was defeated and Hitler of Germany was defeated. After the war, the Japanese did not have many working manufacturing plants going again to make metal things, so they bought all of the old tin cans, coffee cans, bean cans and even Prince Albert tobacco cans they could. They bought them from American junk dealers, took them to Japan and used them to make new things. In Japan, they would cut open the tin cans and flatten out the metal and print new patterns for toys like these little cars. Then they would stamp out the little cars with die-cutting machines, bend and fold them to form a new little car. They did not paint the inside of the metal car because paint is very expensive. That is why you can see words inside. Times were very tough in Japan after the war, but they used their ingenuity to get ahead again."

"What is ingenuity?" asked Luke. The peddler looked across the valley, and said, "It means being clever, or creative in a new way. A small example of ingenuity is these little cars. The Japanese bought up used tin and turned it in to something new again. Does that help to explain it?"

"Oh, I get it, thanks," said Luke. "Remember, don't throw away anything that someone else might use again," said the peddler.

Clay, Luke and Sally Jane were impressed with the old man's knowledge. "Keep the three cars," he said "and we will figure out how you can pay for them before I leave. Now, I would like to speak with your Mama, Sally Jane."

They led him to Sally Jane's cabin and her Mama came to the door. Sally Jane introduced her to the peddler. "He is a smart man, Mama. He told us some really interesting things."

Mama looked at the old man in tattered clothes and no shoes. She was not so sure if she should invite him in. "You kids come into the cabin," she said as she held the screen door open for the peddler.

"Don't be concerned about me, ma'am. I am a harmless old man who has seen better days. I used to peddle these country ridges and knew many of the people up here, all good people, God-fearing people who would give you the shirt off their backs. I was a regular, year after year. All the women on the mountain counted on me for their kitchen wares and the kids counted on me for some little toy play-pretties. About 15 years ago, I got very sick and had to be hospitalized for a number of years so I had to give up peddling. It was several years after the war was over before I finally recovered and could to try peddling again. These days a lot of people have cars, or catch rides to town with someone, so they buy most of what they need in town. That of course hurts my business."

The kids were watching him and could see tears welling up in his eyes. He quit talking for a minute or so, then he said, "I have cataracts now and it

152

sometimes makes my eyes water. He wiped a small tear rolling down his cheek. My old shoes gave out on me a few miles back, but like these kids, I like to go barefoot in the summer. Would you like to see what I have in my bag?"

Naturally Sally Jane's Mama had to say yes, so he started to pull things from his bag; pots and pans, boxes of matches, sore muscle liniments, hair tonic and a set of beautiful hairbrushes. Sally Jane and her mama both eyed the lovely brushes. The peddler saw their expression and could tell this was a winner.

"How much are they, Sir?" Aunt Olive asked.

"They are $1.50 for the set, or you can buy one for 50 cents."

"I am not sure I can pay that much, as we are a little short on money," said Aunt Olive.

Luke looked at Clay. Clay looked at Luke and they said to the peddler, "Would you please come outside with us so we can show you something."

The peddler slowly got up and followed the two boys. When they were out of earshot, they said to the peddler, "We have some money saved. We want to buy the set of 3 brushes and we will give one to Sally Jane, one to Aunt Olive and one to our Mama." They ran to their cabin to get their money and returned.

Sally Jane and her Mama stood looking out of the window and tried to figure out what was going on.

The boys took the set of hairbrushes and chose one for their Mama and then told Sally Jane and Aunt Olive to choose one for each of them. Sally Jane and her Mama grabbed the boys and gave them both a tremendous hug. Everybody was happy, including the peddler.

A little later Mama came walking up the dirt road after work. She saw Clay, Luke and Sally Jane sitting on the porch with some older man that she did not recognize.

As she got closer, she suddenly remembered this old man. "Oscar, is that you? said Mama.

The old man smiled his toothless grin and said, "Yes ma'am, it is me after all these years. The last time I saw you, you were a new bride with no children." They both laughed and she gave Oscar a big hug.

She looked him over and could see how the years had worn away at the younger man she used to know. She could see that he needed better clothes and shoes.

She said, "Oscar, we have a lot to talk about. Pa will be home soon and I know he will want you to spend the night with us."

Mama then motioned for the boys to come inside with her. She told them she knew it was not Saturday, but she wanted them to heat up the water heater outside the bath shed.

She said, "Oscar needs a good bath and we will give him some of Pa's old clothes. I think there is an old pair of Pa's shoes that might fit."

The boys agreed and ran to the back of the shed to build a fire under the water heater.

When they had the fire roaring, they came in and told Oscar that they had a new improvement that they had made and wanted him to try it. They took him to the tub room and asked if he would like to have a nice warm bath.

He did not know what to say. Tears welled up in his eyes, and he said he would be ever so grateful for a bath. The boys told him that they had some clean clothes that he could put on after his bath. His eyes brightened and he gave a huge toothless grin.

Outside the tub room, the boys could hear him humming a song, as he soaked in the warm tub. About a half hour later, he came out of the room looking like a different man. His hair was washed and combed; he had the fresh shirt and pants that the boys had given him. The pants were a bit big but he pulled the belt tight to hold them up. Then they brought him a pair of Pa's old shoes and they fit him perfectly.

The boys looked out the cabin window and saw Doc's old truck dropping Pa by the mailbox. They ran out to meet him and told him the news about Oscar. They told him not to be surprised when he saw Oscar wearing some of his old clothes.

Pa came in and was happy to see Oscar after so many years. He insisted that Oscar spend the night, "but you'll have to sleep in the attic with the boys." Clay said he and Luke could make a pallet on the floor to sleep on so that Oscar could have their bed all to himself.

After a delicious supper, Mama, Pa and Oscar talked long into the night as the two boys listened intently. They learned that Oscar used to be a salesman for a big dry goods company before the Depression in 1929. At that time, like many men, he lost his job and tried to do the only work he knew how to do; by selling things as a country peddler.

After many stories, everyone went to bed. Before long, Luke was snoring and so was Oscar.

Clay was not. He tried to listen for the panther to scream in the mountain, but the loud snoring of the two of them wiped out all other sounds. Clay finally slipped into a deep sleep.

The next morning, everyone awoke to the smell of fresh biscuits, bacon and eggs and fresh fried apple pies.

Oscar rolled over, and said, "Am I in Heaven?" The boys laughed and said, "No, but we are sure no one in Heaven can cook as good as our Mama. Lets go down for breakfast!"

After breakfast, Oscar said he was going to go on up through the mountain trails and roads to other cabins to sell his wares. Before he left, Sally Jane and her mama came over to say goodbye. Oscar said, "I want you kids to have the play-pretties that I gave you yesterday as a gift." Then he reached into his bag and pulled out more gifts; two beautiful tablecloths for the women and a new pocketknife for Pa.

As he left, he waved goodbye and slowly but proudly walked up the trail with his washed hair, clean body, new clothes and a real pair of shoes.

For some time, the kids watched the trail to see if he would come up the mountain again, but he never did. They never saw nor heard from Oscar again.

CHAPTER 21

PARACHUTES IN THE SKY

"Luke, wake up!" called Clay. "I have a great idea. It came to me in a dream last night. Wake up so I can tell you!"

Luke rolled over in his bed and tried to understand what Clay was saying. "Okay, I'm *trying* to wake up. Tell me your dream," said Luke.

"I dreamed that the war was still going, but you and I were the ages we are now. We were sitting in our tree house when we heard a lot of army planes flying over the valley. All of a sudden, there were lots of men jumping out of the airplanes, and their parachutes opened. They all started to float down to the valley towards town when I woke up! So I don't know if they were friend or foe. I am so mad that I woke up when I did. I wish I could have dreamed more."

"So that's it?" said Luke. He rolled over to go back to sleep.

"Wait, Luke, don't go back to sleep! I have more to tell you about what I'm thinking. We should make our own paratroopers and float them down into the valley!"

Luke rolled back over to face Clay. Now he was more interested. "Tell me what you mean."

After breakfast, the boys headed up the hill to Sally Jane's house to tell her about their plan.

Clay said, "We need some old pieces of cloth, like old bed sheet material, and we need some string."

"What are we making?" asked Sally Jane.

"We are going to make little parachutes to throw off the cliff into the wind. We can watch them float into the valley, like they are all soldiers on a mission in the war," said Clay.

"Yeah, Clay dreamed about it last night, and now we are going make his dream come true," said Luke. "Isn't it exciting?

Sally Jane and Luke were not sure how these parachutes would work but they were willing to try it. Clay told them that first they had to find supplies. "We will ask our mamas for some old cloth, Luke and I already have kite string . . . oh, and we need a pair of scissors, so let's get everything together and go up in the tree house to make the parachutes," said Clay.

A little while later, they climbed into the tree house with their supplies. Clay remembered to bring a pencil and paper, as well. He drew his plan for the other two to see. He drew a one-foot square, and then a picture of strings, about a foot long, tied to each corner. Next he illustrated how to tie the ends of the four strings together. Clay realized that each parachute would need a weight so the wind would billow them out and make them float.

Clay said. "What can we use for a weight?"

"Would stones work?" asked Sally Jane.

"No, they would be hard to tie on," said Clay.

"How about those old fishing sinkers that Pa found at the dump?" said Luke. "They're made to attach to fishing line to weight it down under the water, and we need them to weight the parachutes gently down to the earth!"

"Perfect!" said Clay. So Luke ran to the shed and brought back a dozen.

They cut the cloth, tied on the strings, secured the weights and decided to try launching a few into the wind from the tree house.

"Wait!" said Sally Jane; "We should put a note on each one to tell where we sent them from."

"And," said Luke, "let's include our return address in case they fly far away and people want to contact us."

"Great idea, Luke," said Clay, "But they may only drift a short distance."

They wrote notes that said "This parachute was launched on July 19, 1951, by C.L.&SJ Flight Company," and put their return address on them.

They rolled the parachutes into tight balls. Clay threw the first one off the tree house deck. After the wind carried it way out, it opened up and floated down into the valley below, where it was caught by another wind gust and carried so far that the kids couldn't see it anymore. "WOW! It worked!" they all screamed.

The first launch was a big success! Then each of the kids took turns throwing the other parachutes. They watched with joy as they glided on the winds, some only a short distance, others carried further by stronger gusts.

After the launch, they went into the cabin to make peanut butter and muscadine jelly sandwiches. They sat on the front porch of the cabin, ate their sandwiches and fantasized about where their "army" landed and who might find the paratroopers. Would they read the notes and send messages back to them?"

The next day, they watched for the mailman's old Nash car to come chugging up the mountain. When it was finally in view, they jumped down from the tree house and ran to the mailbox hoping for a response from someone.

As the mailman, Old Joe, pulled his car to a stop, they all shouted, "Do you have any mail for C.L.&SJ Flight Company?"

Old Joe said, "No, but guess what? One of your parachutes floated down into my garden yesterday afternoon. My wife looked out the window and saw it coming out of the corner of her eye. At first she thought it was a real parachute and paratrooper, but then realized it was much smaller and closer than she first thought. She yelled for me to come see and we watched it float into the garden. We went out to pick it up and when I read the note I figured it had to be you three!"

"Wow, hot diggity dog," said Clay, and all three of them beamed!

Old Joe said, "I brought it back so you can launch it again."

"Thanks," they said.

"Who knows, you might get some letters in the mail from the folks that find the others," said Old Joe. "I called the town newspaper and talked with the editor about what you kids are doing. He said it sounded like a good story for his paper, so he just might be coming up to talk to you about it."

"Oh, my," said Sally Jane. "We have never been in the newspaper before. Do you think he will take our photograph to put in the paper?"

"I would not be surprised. Readers love to see pictures of the people in a story," said Old Joe.

He said goodbye and the kids watched the old Nash pull away.

They ran to the cabin, screaming, "We might get our photographs in the town newspaper!" Pa came from behind the cabin, Aunt Olive came running down the hill and Mama came hurrying out of the cabin. They all wanted to know what the kids were screaming about.

Clay, Sally Jane and Luke sat on the porch and told their parents about the entire adventure, starting with Clay's dream. They hoped their parachutes would be found and that they would hear from the people who found them. They also told of their hope that the editor of the paper would interview them.

"Then we will have 'celebrities' in the family," said Pa with a smile.

"Well, we'll just wait and see," said Luke.

That afternoon, the kids watched the valley road from the tree house, but the editor of the paper never came. They went to bed that night hoping that tomorrow he would.

The next day, they watched again and saw the mailman's old Nash chug up the hill. Behind him was a big black car that the kids did not recognize.

The mailman pulled up to the mailbox, but this time he got out of his car and said he had two more letters for C.L.&SJ Flight Company. He also said that he had the editor of the paper follow him so he could introduce him to the kids. They were thrilled, and a little bit nervous.

The editor got out of his car with a pad of paper in his hand. He said he heard about their adventure and wanted to write an article about the entire story.

He saw the mailman hand them some mail and he asked, "Are these letters from people who found your parachutes? If they are, please open them and read 'em to us."

Mama, Pa and Aunt Olive saw that something was happening down at the mailbox, so they all came to listen.

The first letter was from a farmer across town that found the parachute in his newly plowed field. He said he guessed that C.L.&SJ Flight Company was from kids so he was enclosing a dollar bill and said it was a little gift to thank them for the joy it brought him. It reminded him of his own boyhood and the thrill he got out of inventing his own toys.

The second letter was from a man far away in Nashville. He said he was driving on the highway in eastern Tennessee, day before yesterday, and when he got back to Nashville, he noticed something hooked onto the bed of his truck. Looking closer, he discovered the parachute. It apparently caught the back of his truck as it settled down from the sky.

"These are great stories," said the editor. All the kids grinned. Luke's eyes were as big as saucers and Sally Jane wiped away a tear of joy. The editor said he wanted to get the camera from his car to take a photograph of the kids, the tree house, and the cabins they live in. Then he wanted a picture of the whole family. Everyone got nervous that their clothes were not nice enough for a picture in the newspaper, but the editor said that their honest appearance added strength to the story.

First, he took a photo of the kids holding one of their parachutes and the two letters that had come in the mail. The editor was a big man, but he finally made it up into the tree house to take pictures of the kids lying in the tree house looking down into the valley below. He also snapped a picture of the entire family, and finally he took a photo of the kids and the mailman.

Then the editor got into his car and left. They were thrilled that he wanted to publish their story. The mailman was about to leave when Mama asked if he could come in for some sweet tea, but he said no, he had already spent a lot of time and the people on his mail route needed to have their mail.

Old Joe waved goodbye as he drove off and said, "I hope that tomorrow I will have more mail for C.L.&SJ." They all felt proud.

The next few days brought a few more letters from local folk. Then, one day, Old Joe came honking his horn.

The kids came running. "What is it?" they yelled.

Old Joe said he had a special delivery letter for them from the new television station in Knoxville!

Mama, Pa and Aunt Olive heard the honking, so they came running too.

Excitedly, they carefully tore open the envelope and it said:

"We have heard about your amazing flight experiment and your parachutes. We believe it would be a great human-interest story for our evening news. Would you allow our team to come to your home and interview you? Please let us know soon. Thank you.

Samuel Cook, Editor
'Nightly News, Channel 6, Knoxville."

"Oh my goodness, oh my goodness!" exclaimed Sally Jane. Clay and Luke were speechless.

They had read about this new thing called television in "The Weekly Reader" (a newspaper just for kids) at school. But the only television show that Clay, Luke and Sally Jane had seen was at Doyle's hardware store in town. There was a very tall antenna on the roof of the store so they could get reception from Knoxville, fifty miles away. It was the only TV in town and since the store had it in the front store window, people could gather outside to watch it.

"If you want to answer the letter while I continue on my mail route, I will stop again on my way back to town and pick it up. The television station will probably get your letter day after tomorrow."

That seemed like a good idea, so for the next two hours, they tried to figure out what they should say in their letter to the station.

Pa finally said, "Just say: YES, WE WOULD LOVE TO HAVE YOU INTERVIEW US! That's all you need to say." So that's exactly what they wrote.

A few hours later, Old Joe stopped by to pick up the letter.

After Sally Jane and Aunt Olive went home, Clay and Luke had supper with Mama and Pa. They talked about the television people coming all the way into the mountains to interview them at their little cabin.

"We're going to be famous!" exclaimed Clay. "Everyone in town reads the weekly newspaper and I'm sure our story will spread to the radio, too."

"Maybe they will interview us, too," said Luke.

"Now, we don't want you to get a big head about this," said Pa. "Mama and I are as excited as you are, but we have got to stay our sweet selves, okay?"

They understood, but the boys could not wait until morning to ride their bikes up Panther Creek Road to tell the neighbors, especially Georgie. "We will have to explain the TV to Georgie, because he has not yet seen the television at the hardware store. He only understands radio," said Clay.

They said goodnight and climbed the ladder to their room. Both boys had trouble going sleep. They were each wondering what to say when the TV people started interviewing them. Finally Luke was snoring, and Clay waited to hear the panther scream.

After a long time, just as he was falling asleep, he heard the blood-curdling scream, but this time it sounded much nearer to the neighborhood.

He heard the neighbor's dogs barking furiously further up the road from his cabin.

He wondered if Sally Jane heard it, too. Then he fell asleep.

CHAPTER 22

MORE LETTERS ARRIVE

Clay, Luke and Sally Jane waited anxiously each day for the mailman to arrive. They received two more letters from people who found their parachutes.

One letter was from Mrs. Bookreader, the town librarian. She'd found one of the parachutes in her front yard. In her letter, she asked Clay, Luke and Sally Jane if they would be so kind as to do a parachute class in one of the library's presentation rooms, to demonstrate how to make them. She said that she could pay them $5.00 for the class, if they were interested.

"Interested?" shouted Clay, "Mrs. Bookreader can bet her last dime we are!"

"YES!" Said Luke and Sally Jane, "We are very interested!"

"We have started a business of our own, but are we businessmen or teachers?" asked Luke. They laughed and said, "Both!"

They watched for the mailman's old Nash car as he returned to town after his mail route. They flagged him down and ask if he could take a letter to the librarian in town so she would get it today. He said he would be glad to.

They could not wait until supper to tell their parents the news.

"We have to start thinking about how we do a class for kids," said Clay. "What if I do the introduction and the main talking and you two hand out the supplies and be ready to help any child who needs it?"

"Wow, you are already sounding like a teacher, using words like 'any child,'" said Luke as he laughed. Sally Jane laughed too.

"Where are we going to get the supplies?" asked Sally Jane.

"We will ask the Mrs. Bookreader if we can charge each child twenty-five cents for materials. Then we will ask our Mamas for more old bed sheets that we can cut up for the parachutes. We already have a lot of string and sinkers, so we can make some more money selling our parachute kits," said Clay.

"Boy, am I impressed with your business sense, Clay," said Sally Jane. Luke just stood there wishing he had been the one to come up with the idea.

Sally Jane could see that Luke looked a bit left out, so she said, "I have two of the cutest, smartest cousins in the world!" Clay and Luke both blushed and Luke brightened up.

The next day, two important letters arrived. The first was from Mrs. Bookreader agreeing to all their requests, but the most exciting one was from the television station in Knoxville.

Dear Clay, Sally Jane and Luke,

I am delighted that you have agreed to let us interview you. I am sending one of my reporters, Sam Francis, to your place on Panther Creek Road next Monday. He will have several people with him—a cameraman, a soundman and a producer. The crew will have about an hour to spend at your home, so it would be nice if your Mama would have some fresh sweet tea prepared for them when they arrive.

We are aware that there is no electrical power in your community, so you do not have televisions. We are sending a special request to Mr. Doyle to invite the community to his store on the night the story will be broadcast. That way everyone can see the news about you and your interesting idea. We are sure that you and your family will want to be there as well.

Again, I want to thank you for sharing your adventure with our viewers.

Sincerely,
Samuel Cook, Editor
Channel 6 News, Knoxville, Tennessee

Aunt Olive and Sally Jane came for supper. They were all excited and talking a mile a minute. Mama said that she and Aunt Olive would certainly make fresh sweet tea for the crew, as well as sugar cookies and a blackberry cobbler. The kids and Pa said they would rake the yard and repair the front steps. They wanted the place to look good.

Everybody had trouble going to sleep that night, including Aunt Olive and Sally Jane up in their cabin.

On this night, they were all awake when the panther screamed.

CHAPTER 23

THE TV TRUCK IS COMING UP THE MOUNTAIN!

"Clay, Wake Up! We've overslept and it is 7 O'clock!" yelled Luke. "Today's the day that the TV people are coming, so we have to hurry."

"It's not that late," said Clay, "why all the hurry?"

"Well, we have to get our faces washed and our hair combed and have on clean clothes and make sure that Sally Jane is ready too," said Luke.

The sun was shining through the boy's attic window. It was a warm summer day. A breeze was softly blowing through the evergreen trees in the yard.

Mama called up and said, "You two '*TV stars*' had better come down and eat your breakfast."

They were just finishing breakfast when Sally Jane came running through the door. She did not have on her overalls as usual. She had on a blue summer dress and her beautiful ponytail was tied with a big blue satin ribbon.

"Wow," said Clay. "Where did you come from, Miss?" They all laughed. "Can you climb up into the tree house in that dress? We have to go and watch for the TV truck coming up the mountain, you know."

"Yes. I know, and I can certainly shimmy up a tree in a dress as easily as in shorts or overalls. You boys will just have to go up the tree first."

They were in the tree house when they saw a plume of dust trailing a service van through the valley and then it turned up Panther Creek Road. They all shouted to Mama, Pa an Aunt Olive, "HERE THEY COME!"

Soon the kids were on the ground, standing by the road as the truck pulled up. "We are looking for C.L.&SJ Company," said the driver. He had a grin on his face. "Could that possibly be you three?" he asked, again grinning.

"Yes, we are C.L.&SJ," said Luke. "Welcome."

Clay introduced the family and the man driving the truck said he was the reporter, Sam Francis, then he introduced Fred, the cameraman, George, the soundman and Lucy, the producer. Lucy had beautiful, long, blonde hair. Clay, Luke and Sally Jane could not take their eyes off of her. They had never seen such a beauty on this mountain.

Lucy took over and explained how they were going to shoot the scenes. She said, "First we want to show the view of the valley and then a view around the cabin to set the scene for our viewers. Then Sam Francis will ask you his questions. After that, we will take a break. Our boss told us you just might have some sweet tea for us."

"Oh, yes we do!" said Mama and Aunt Olive in unison. Clay could see that they were a bit nervous. Pa just stood in back and watched with a smile.

Luke looked around and said, "Wow! The yard is full of people!" All the neighbors came to watch the greatest excitement this ridge had ever seen. He noticed that the town's weekly newspaper editor was there as well. He waved to him.

The cameras and sound equipment were taken from the truck and set up in the yard. Floodlights were set up too, even though it was daylight.

Ol' man Hickie, a neighbor from up the ridge, said, "Dad gum, this here's just like Hollywood, Californi-ay, and I am sure that there pretty blonde one over yonder is a movie star." Everyone laughed.

The crew got some great shots of the valley from the deck of the tree house, as well as views around the cabin, including the "Hot Baths" room and the the water spring up the hill behind the cabin.

"Where is your outhouse?" asked Sam Francis.

"Do you want a picture of it, too?" asked Pa, surprised.

"No," answered Sam, "I just need to go to the toilet." Again everyone snickered.

The next fifteen minutes were spent answering many questions, like:

How did you come up with the parachute idea?

Have you studied aeronautics?

Where did you get the material to make the chutes?

How did you get them to fly so far? We heard one of them was found in Nashville.

We hear you are going to teach a class at the Library. Tell us about it.

Do any of you think you might want to be an air force pilot someday?

Then Lucy said, "Time for a break." They all relaxed and had sweet tea and blackberry cobbler. Mama showed them through the cabin and they were very gracious and said, "How lovely and quaint."

Clay, Luke and Sally Jane all looked at each other and wondered, 'What does quaint mean?' But they said nothing.

After the break, there were more questions. Lucy told the family to get together for a family shot. They all did, smiling, except Pa who was trying to not show his snaggled teeth.

After a couple of shots, Luke said, "Lucy, could we kids have our picture taken with you?"

Clay was shocked that Luke would be so bold as to ask the beautiful woman if she would have her picture taken with them.

She said, "I would love to! Luke, you stand on one side of me, and Clay on the other. Sally Jane you stand in front of me. I will put my arms around you and the boys can put their arms around me."

The two boys about died, turning as red as beets in the summer. They were thrilled, but scared nearly to death at the same time. Mama had her Kodak camera and rushed up to get a photo. This was too good to miss.

The interview was over, and the truck was packed. Lucy gave each of the three kids a big hug and waved goodbye as the truck started down the mountain.

The town newspaper editor came up to congratulate them and introduced them to Tim Smith, the owner of the radio station in town. He told them he would like to interview them on his radio station next week.

"Great," they said. "We will be happy to."

After everyone left, they were so excited they started doing cartwheels in the yard. Sally Jane said, "Remember when the reporter asked if we wanted to be Air Force pilots some day? Well I almost said, YES, I DO! I was afraid he might not know what to think, me being a girl. I am sure he was addressing you two boys. But do you know what? I just might be the first girl pilot someday!"

Aunt Olive and Mama clapped.

Pa just looked shocked.

Clay and Luke just looked at each other and each knew what the other was thinking: *'Yes, we are sure she just might be.'*

Then supper was served, fried potatoes with white gravy, fried okra, cornbread and lots of blackberry cobbler.

After the dishes were washed Clay said, "We are all so wound up with excitement that I am sure none of us can go to sleep for a while. So, Sally Jane and Aunt Olive, please stay for a while and let's play dominos."

Before they started playing games, Pa said, "I sure hope that camera can photograph the color red, Clay, because you and Luke turned bright red when Lucy told you two to put your arms around her waist."

Sally Jane, Aunt Olive, Mama and Pa started laughing. Clay and Luke blushed, but everyone could tell that they had loved it.

They played dominos late into the night, and then they heard the panther scream.

Clay and Luke said they would walk the women home.

When they got to Aunt Olive's door, Sally Jane ran over and gave the boys a big hug. "This day has been a wonderful adventure! Thanks, Clay and Luke!" This time they did not blush. They were starting to get used to it.

CHAPTER 24

THE TV SHOW

"Tonight's the night!" exclaimed Clay, "We are going to be on television!" The editor of the newspaper promised to send his big black car to take the family to town, and 'Doc' said he would haul everyone else from the ridge to the newscast at Doyle's Hardware Store in the bed of his old truck.

"The back of Doc's truck will be full since everyone on the ridge wants to see the kids on TV," said Pa. Everyone was jumping out of their skin with excitement.

Sally Jane, Clay and Luke tried to keep busy all day so that time would pass by faster.

At about 5:00, they saw the big black car coming up the mountain. The kids and their folks were ready and waiting to get in when it arrived, so they all piled in the big car. It was so different from "Doc's" old Model A pickup. They could not believe how big, roomy, and plush it was.

It was about a fifteen-minute ride to town, but it seemed like an hour to the kids because they were so anxious to get there.

When the car pulled up to the hardware store, a crowd had already gathered. Chairs had been set up for the "special guests" outside. The rest of the people had to stand, but no one cared.

The kids and their family were ushered to their seats. They had never been honored like this before, and felt a bit embarrassed by the attention.

It was nearly time for the newscast to begin. The hardware store workers were trying their best to get a sharp picture on the black and white television set and make sure the outdoor speakers were turned up loud enough so all could hear. Finally the picture was clear and the editor of the paper introduced the three kids, Clay, Sally Jane and Luke. The crowd hooted and hollered.

The newscast came on the TV and the announcer told what was going to be on the news. He said, "We have three special guests tonight, young people from Panther Creek Ridge, away up in the mountains. They have an amazing story for you." Again, everyone hooted and hollered.

Finally it was time for the story that everyone was waiting for. People were crowded in closer to the window of the store. No one wanted to miss anything.

Everyone laughed when the picture of Clay, Sally Jane and Luke appeared on the TV. The kids didn't know what to think of seeing themselves from different angles on the screen. Luke had his hands in his front pockets and seemed to be trying to scratch himself without anyone noticing. When the crowd saw it, everyone laughed and giggled, except Luke. He was a bit embarrassed.

Near the end of the telecast, there was a picture of the whole family, and everybody cheered. Then at the end the news, when there was a picture of four of their parachutes floating across the TV screen, everyone cheered even louder!

Finally, the TV was switched off and the editor asked each of the three kids to say a few words. Clay told how he dreamed up the idea. Luke told how they made the parachutes and Sally Jane told of the letters they had received, then she said, "We all love the idea of flying things, and someday, I want to be the first woman pilot in the Air Force."

There were murmurs of surprise and a few startled expressions hearing that a girl would think this way. One older man said, "Young lady, that is men's work. You should be happy to be a good housewife and mother."

Sally Jane replied, "Sir, I don't mean to be disrespectful. I do want to be a housewife and mother someday, but I think I want to be a pilot first."

All the young girls applauded her bravery and her respectful manner. The boys in the crowd were not sure what they should do. Then one of them joined the applause, and the others joined in.

Clay announced that there would be a class on making parachutes on Sunday afternoon at the library and that everyone was welcomed to attend.

Lots of people huddled around the kids to congratulate them and ask for autographs. Many girls gathered around Clay, giggling. Luke looked a bit jealous.

Young boys started sidling up to Sally Jane to ask for her autograph. She was flattered and told them she would love to. She signed each boy's paper and drew a smile on each. The boys were thrilled.

Then she spotted some shy young girls, about Luke's age. She went over to them and asked if they might like to have Luke's autograph. They giggled and said yes, so she took them over to him. Luke's eyes got big and his face turned as red as a plum. He signed for each girl and they jumped up and down and giggled some more.

Eventually the excitement died down, and the big black car took them back up the mountain. "Doc" followed in his truck filled with neighbors. Most had never seen a TV before, so it had been a big evening for everyone.

They thanked the editor for his help and asked him if he would like to come in for some sweet tea. He declined and said he needed to get home.

The kids and family climbed the steps to the cabin porch and sat and discussed the events of the day. Everyone told their favorite part. Pa said he was concerned that the old men in town were going to tease him when they saw him and call him a TV star. They all laughed. They could tell that he loved the attention!

After everyone told their story, it was pretty late. Clay and Luke walked Aunt Olive and Sally Jane to their cabin. As they approached the front steps, they heard the panther scream.

Clay said it sounded like it was time for everyone to be in bed. Luke was happy that he was awake tonight to hear the panther scream.

The boys said goodnight and then they ran home as fast as their legs could carry them making sure there was no panther hot on their heels.

CHAPTER 25

THE MOUND IN THE WOODS

One morning when things were getting back to normal, Clay suggested that the three of them spend the day exploring the woods. Sally Jane made sandwiches, Luke made sweet tea and got Mama to contribute sugar cookies she had just baked, hot out of the oven. They were excited about another a new adventure, although no one yet knew what the adventure might be.

The boys and Sally Jane jumped on their bikes and headed up Panther Creek Road.

Suddenly, Clay yelled. "I have an idea, let's go see if we can find that old mound in the woods that Luke and I found last year, before you moved here, Sally Jane." Luke agreed and Sally Jane wanted to know more.

"What do you mean by a mound?" said Sally Jane. Clay answered that he and Luke thought it might be an old Indian mound where the dead are buried, or perhaps an Indian camp from many years ago.

Soon they came to the place where the creek ran under the road. They hid their bikes in the bushes and started hiking down to the creek.

In about fifteen minutes Clay said, "I think this it, over that way about 100 feet."

The underbrush was so thick that the kids had to push their way through it. Soon they came to an opening where the trees grew in a circle around a dirt mound covered with grass. It seemed almost spooky, as though they were on a sacred ceremonial space, but nevertheless, it did not look like anyone had been there for years.

They all stopped walking. It was almost noon, so they climbed to the top of the mound to have dinner.

As they sat on the grassy knoll and ate their sandwiches and cookies, Sally Jane asked what they thought the Indians did at the mound.

Clay suggested that it was probably an Indian burial ground, and there could be a hundred Indians buried here.

Luke's eyes got as big as a new moon. "WHAT?" He said, "You mean we might be eating right on top of where someone is buried!"

Just as he said this, they heard a loud scream from a hawk sitting up in a tree above them. The sound scared all three of them half to death, but Clay tried to act brave and said, "Don't be frightened. It is only a hawk sitting up there on that high branch in the tree."

"AND I BET HE IS SUPPOSED TO BE WATCHING OVER THIS BURIAL SITE AND DOES NOT WANT US HERE! I BET HE IS A SPIRIT OF THE DEAD!" Luke shouted.

Sally Jane looked stunned and just sat there.

"Let's leave here, NOW!" said Luke, "Before something bad happens."

Clay said, "Now kids, I think you are over-reacting. Are you two superstitious?" They all agreed they were over-reacting and decided they would stay and explore the area.

As they were finishing their sandwiches, Clay caught a glimpse of something half-buried in the grass. He looked closer and realized it was an arrowhead. This excited everyone.

Clay suggested that they get on their knees and crawl around and look closely in the grass to see if they could find anything that looked like it had belonged to the Indians.

In a few minutes, Luke yelled, "Hey, I just found another arrowhead, and it is beautiful!"

Clay and Sally Jane ran over to see. They were overjoyed, because finding two arrowheads meant that there were probably more around here. As they crawled around, they dug with their fingers, scratching into the dirt. Soon they found more arrowheads and shards of old pottery. They took the empty cloth dinner sack and put the treasures inside it.

Every few minutes the Hawk would scream out his warning that they were not wanted there. Each time they heard it, it shook them up a bit more.

"I hope he does not fly down and try to peck our eyes out," said Sally Jane. They all started to keep an eye on the hawk, but he never swept down on them.

Clay, looked at the sun in the sky and said, "I think it is time to head home."

As they walked back to the road they all agreed that this new discovery must be kept secret. They did not want other kids coming and digging for Indian artifacts. They all promised and crossed their hearts that they would not tell.

As they arrived home, they knew that they would have to tell the parents because the parents would want to know where the treasures had been found. They would wait until tomorrow to show their parents the treasures and to ask them to keep their secret.

When Luke and Clay crawled into bed, Clay said he wondered if they dug down further into the mound, they might find Indian skeletons.

Luke sat straight up in his bed and said, "You're not serious, are you, Clay?"

Clay laughed and said, "No, I just wanted to see your reaction."

That night Luke could not go to sleep, thinking about digging up old skeletons. He lay awake for a long time. Then he heard the panther scream up in the mountain.

"Hey, Clay!" he said excited, "I heard the panther!"

Clay said nothing; for a change, he was sound asleep, with a smile on his face.

CHAPTER 26
TELLING ABOUT FINDING THE MOUND

Early the next morning, Luke woke Clay. "Clay, wake up—we have to talk." Clay was sound asleep and tried to open his eyes to see why his little brother was bothering him. Luke said, "I had a terrible nightmare that we were digging in the Indian mound and the hawk was in the tree screaming. All of a sudden the ground opened up and we fell down in the grave with the skeletons! It was horrible, and the hawk was just screaming like he was laughing at us, and then I woke up scared. Promise that you will not tell anyone I was scared, okay?" "Promise I won't," said Clay, feeling a little guilty about scaring Luke about the skeletons. In a few minutes Luke said that he was okay now. They got up and went down for breakfast.

After breakfast they told Mama and Pa that Sally Jane and Aunt Olive were coming over because they had a secret to tell the parents. Pa's eyes got big and quizzical, but he did not say anything.

They heard footsteps on the front porch, and Sally Jane and Aunt Olive came inside. Sally Jane had a sheepish look on her face. Clay said, "We have a new discovery we made yesterday, but we do not want you to tell anybody, okay?" We were up in the deep woods and found what we think is an old Indian mound. It is surrounded with a large circle of trees and the mound rises about four feet above the rest of the earth."

"AND," said Luke, "there is a huge hawk that sits in one of the trees and screams out at us like we are not supposed to be there."

"Guess what else?" said Sally Jane. "We found some nice arrowheads and broken shards of old pottery."

"We want to go back up there with a shovel and dig down deeper and see what we can find," said Clay.

Luke exclaimed, " And! Clay tried to scare me by telling me we might find old Indian skeletons!"

"That could be true," said Pa. "It might be a human grave, or it might be a grave for an Indian horse or horses. Who knows? But I will tell you something that the old timers way up in the mountain believe, or claim to, and that is if you dig around in an Indian grave of any kind, you will be haunted by their dead spirits, day and night for the rest of your days. I don't know if it is true, but I would never want to find out, would you? There are a lot of old tales that have been passed down from generation to generation. Some men swear them to be true. You might think about it before you go back up there and start digging."

The kids looked dumbstruck. They just sat still, frozen in place, until finally Clay spoke. "Do you think the spirits, if there really are some, would be angry that we picked up the arrowheads and broken pottery, Pa? We could take them back and put the pieces where we found them if you think that is best."

Pa looked at the three of them and said that he thought the mound might be sacred ground to some people. He said, "We should honor their beliefs and show respect. I am not going to tell you what to do. You are all old enough to think seriously about this."

They all looked at each other, and said, "We will return the arrowheads and shards this afternoon." A look of relief came over their faces. Mama and Aunt Olive said they agreed with Pa about respecting the dead and their culture.

Pa told them that if they find any arrowheads while walking through the woods or down in the valley in a plowed field, that they could keep those. Indians hunting years ago probably left them behind.

After dinner, they rode their bikes back up the road, walked into the woods until they found the mound. The hawk flew into the tree as they approached and watched them carefully. He did not scream this time. They dropped the artifacts back on the mound, and gently pushed them into the grass. They all stood solemnly for a moment. No one said anything.

As they turned to go, the hawk flew in a large circle above them, and then landed back in the tree. He watched them as they headed toward home. He was silent.

CHAPTER 27

SUMMER IS ALMOST OVER!

Summer was almost over, although none of the kids wanted it to end. There were still more adventures to have.

When they met under the big oak tree to discuss what they were going to do, Clay said, "I think we should build a cart that will hold all three of us. We can ride it down the hill on Panther Creek Road. Remember, we found four small bike wheels at the dump a while back and I think they will be perfect." Luke and Sally Jane immediately agreed that the idea was a good one. "What do we need to build it besides the four wheels?" asked Sally Jane. Luke spoke up and said, "Clay and I have built carts before you moved here, Sally Jane, so we know what we need; a long, heavy board for the main frame, two short boards, two axles and three trike seats."

I think we can find everything we need behind the shed. A little later, they had gathered everything together. First they attached the axles to the short boards, and then used long nails to nail the short boards to the long one. They put the four wheels on the axles, and attached the three old trike seats they had also found at the dump. The last thing was to attach the rope so they could steer the cart.

When they were finished, they all stood back and admired their work. "Do you think it might fall apart with three of us on it?" asked Sally Jane. "Oh, this will hold a ton," said Clay, "so don't worry." He sounded confident.

They pulled the cart down the road to where it went sharply downhill.. "Are we all ready for the adventure of our lives?" said Clay. Luke's eyes got big with excitement. Sally Jane jumped up and down and said, "LETS GO! LETS GO!" Her ponytail glistened in the sunshine.

Clay said he should be the driver of the cart since he was the oldest. Luke told Sally Jane to sit on the second seat and he would ride on the third one. They all climbed on. "If we start going too fast and lose control, everyone drag their feet on the road to help slow us down, okay?" said Clay. They said they would.

The cart started to roll down the hill and then started to pick up more speed. "Should we drag our feet yet?" yelled Luke. "No, I have everything under control," yelled Clay. The cart started to go even faster as they rounded the sharp curve in the road. "OH, NO" yelled Clay! He saw old man Ramus coming up the hill toward them in his wagon, pulled by his old half-blind horse, Jake.

Clay screamed, "Put down your feet and drag them hard!" Sally Jane and Luke also saw the wagon and the horse coming right at them on the narrow road, but neither old man Ramus nor the horse had seen them. The old man was almost blind, too.

The cart started to weave back and forth as the kids dragged their feet. "Hold on for dear life!" yelled Clay, "We have to go into the ditch to miss him!" They all held tight, but the cart hit the side of the ditch and overturned. All three kids spilled into the ditch and skidded along the bottom until finally coming to a stop. They were still a short distance from the old man's wagon. "Anyone hurt?" shouted Clay. "I think I am," groaned Luke.

The old man heard the crash but did not see what happened. "Hey, what's going on?" he yelled. Because the horse could not see, either, the noise of the cart crashing had spooked him and he reared up and almost upset old man Ramus' wagon.

Clay jumped out of the ditch and grabbed the reigns of the horse to try to calm it down. "Mr. Ramus, It is me, Clay. After he calmed the horse, he explained, "We were riding our cart down the hill and tried to stop when we saw you on the road. We are sorry if we scared you and your horse." Sally Jane and Luke let Clay do the talking.

Old man Ramus sat back in his wagon seat and said, "You could have killed us all." Then he smiled a crooked smile and said that he had once been a boy and he used to do foolish things himself. "Where are Luke and Sally Jane?" he said, "They should be in on all this fun."

"They are sitting over there in the ditch," said Clay, "We were all in the wreck."

Oh, I did not see them," said old man Ramus. "You see, my eyesight is not so good anymore and neither are the eyes on my old horse, so we didn't see you coming. Are the other two hurt?"

Before Clay could answer, Luke said, "I hurt my foot, and I'm not sure I can walk on it."

Old man Ramus told Clay and Sally Jane to help Luke get up into his wagon so he would not have to walk. He then told Clay and Sally Jane to tie the cart to his wagon and he would pull it back up the mountain. After they tied the cart, Sally Jane and Clay crawled into the wagon and sat next to Luke.

The ride home was very slow because the old horse moved ever so slowly. When the wagon finally reached their cabin, they helped Luke get down. They apologized to old man Ramus. He said, "That's alright, but I sure could use a glass of water. I am pretty thirsty."

Mama looked out the window and saw the horse and wagon. She came out and asked, "What brings you here, Mr. Ramus? It is nice to see you again." The old man just grinned and said that he had just been part of one of the kid's adventures." Mama saw the dirt all over the kid's clothes, and then she saw Luke limping. "What is this all about?" she asked. "Oh, they had a little accident going down the mountain on their cart, so I gave them a ride home in my wagon," said old man Ramus.

After old man Ramus left with his horse, the kids told Mama the whole story. They felt terrible that they frightened old Man Ramus and his horse. Mama rubbed Sloan's Liniment on Luke's foot and then wrapped it with fresh bandages and said sternly, "My advice to you three would be to figure out a way to attach a brake to your cart before you fly down the hill again." Then she smiled. They were all relieved when she smiled.

CHAPTER 28

OUR SUMMER IS OVER

Sally Jane came running into the yard, her ponytail bouncing and her eyes shining brightly. "Have you boys looked at the calendar lately? It is almost time for school to start and I am so excited."

"I will be going to a new school this year and meeting new kids!" she exclaimed.

Clay and Luke just looked at her. They were not excited that the summer was ending. Summer adventures were over and going barefoot would have to wait until next year.

"Well, we are not that excited," said Clay. "We already know all the kids and we will miss the ridge every day. You, Sally Jane will be the 'Queen of the Party', a new blonde girl with sky-blue eyes."

"Are you a little jealous of your cousin?" Sally Jane asked teasingly.

Clay blushed when he realized that she knew what he was thinking.

"You know that we cousins will stay close to each other, and no one is coming between us," she said. Clay felt better hearing her say this.

"Let's plan a little party with our parents, and maybe some neighbors, to celebrate the end of our summer," said Clay. "Good thinking," said Sally

Jane. "School starts next Monday and that is only four days away!

"Let's start planning," Luke said, "We can ask Pa if he will get his fiddle out of the attic and play some tunes for us."

"And I will play the harmonica," said Sally Jane."

"You can play the harmonica?" both boys said in unison.

"Yes I can, but I have been a bit shy about letting you know."

"That's wonderful! Luke will play spoons and I will play the hair comb," said Clay.

Sally Jane wanted to know what Clay meant by playing a hair comb. The boys both laughed and told her that they discovered that they could take an ordinary hair comb and put wax paper over it. If you put your lips against the wax paper and kind of hum and blow at the same time and you can get a musical sound out of it, similar to a kazoo.

"What if we try singing together?" suggested Clay. "Luke and I sang a duet at church last year and everyone told us we were good. So if you sing, Sally Jane, then we can be a trio." "Oh, I can sing!" she said.

They climbed into the tree house to see how their voices sounded together. They sat on the edge of the tree house deck, and while looking out to the mountains in the distance, Clay started to sing, "Way down South in the Land of Cotton" and the other two joined in. They sounded remarkably good. They all smiled at each other and Luke sang "Yankee Doodle Dandy" and they harmonized with him.

Suddenly, they heard Mama under the tree house saying, "Where is that beautiful music coming from?"

"It's us, Mama" shouted Clay. "How do we sound?"

"I think that with a little practice, the three of you could sing on the radio!" she said.

They told Mama they were thinking about throwing an end-of-summer party.

Mama thought it was a good idea. "We will all sit around and talk about it tonight and make plans."

Sally Jane and Aunt Olive came down for supper, Aunt Olive brought baked beans and Sally Jane brought a chocolate cake she had made. Mama had turnip greens and fried potatoes,

They sat around the table, ate the delicious food and started making plans.

Luke said, "I think we should invite Georgie and his mama and pa."

"Why don't we invite all the neighbors on the ridge? We can ask each of the families to bring snacks for the party, and Pa, you can make your famous sassafras tea," said Mama.

"Then I better start digging some sassafras roots," said Pa.

"We also want to have music for the party. Pa, we want you to get your old fiddle and play, and we can ask old "Doc" Robinson to bring his jaw's harp. In fact let's tell the neighbors to bring any musical instruments they play," said Clay "And we have a surprise for you! The three of us are going to practice between now and Saturday night and we will be a song-singing trio!"

"Wonderful!" said their parents.

So the next day, all three kids wrote out the invitation to the neighbors:

Summer's End Party at the McDougal's House

Saturday night Seven o'clock

OUTSIDE UNDER THE STARS

Bring treats and any musical instrument you have.

McDougals will furnish the drinks.

Every one bring your own chair or cushion.

Music, food, dancing and fun for everyone.

They rode their bikes to each cabin to spread the news. The neighbors were delighted to be invited.

Old Mrs. Smithson said, "You tell your mama that I'm bringing my famous shoo-fly pie."

Every cabin they stopped at offered to bring food and a musical instrument, as well. Ol' Larry Tuffy, the coon hunter, told them the only thing he could play was a saw, and wanted to know if that was okay. The kids all said, "Yes, we will love that!" Larry smiled.

At supper that evening, they reported that every family on the ridge was going to be there. Pa said, "Then I better get to makin' that Sassafras Tea tomorrow. I better have about five gallons, I suspect."

"And we'll set the front porch up as a stage," said Clay. "This is going to be so much fun."

The next two days, the kids practiced singing, Pa worked on some fiddle tunes, Mama started making sounds on an old washtub base that Pa had made, while Aunt Olive practiced her dulcimer. They got the front porch ready by hanging kerosene lamps. In the front yard, they set up a big table made out of old boards for the food and drinks.

Saturday evening came and neighbors began gathering in the front yard. There was a lot of excitement.

Old man Ramus arrived in his buggy pulled by his old blind horse. The old couple, Mrs. and Mr. Smithson, arrived in their wagon. Ol' Larry Tuffy and his wife, Elvira. walked down from their cabin, while Doc, Bonnie Blue and Georgie came in the old Model A ford truck. Then Jensens, who lived over the hill and were seldom seen in the community came riding two old mules, and Tory Smitters, the well digger, walked down the hill with his new girlfriend.

The family had agreed that Clay should be the master of ceremonies. He jumped up onto the front porch and let out a loud whistle to get everyone's attention.

He welcomed and then thanked them for bringing the good food and their wonderful instruments. He said they should eat first and then there will be mountain music all evening. Everyone clapped and cheered.

The neighbors gathered around the large table and were soon scarfing down cakes, pies, cookies, muffins, vanilla wafer pudding and drinking Pa's Famous Sassafras Tea.

The music started with Pa on the fiddle; then everybody with an instrument joined in. Those that did not started dancing across the front yard.

They played washtub bases, scrub boards, dulcimers, tin whistles, jaw's harps, fiddles and even spoons.

The music was wonderful and went on for a while. Then Pa said, "We have a lot of good singers on this ridge, so let's hear from them." Everyone was a bit hesitant to be the first singer, so Sally Jane yelled out, "We have a new group called the 'Panther

Creek Ridge Trio.'" Everyone looked around to see who the trio was.

Clay, Luke and Sally Jane jumped up on the porch and started to sing with Pa accompanying them. The crowd was astonished! Their harmony was breathtaking. At the end of the song, the neighbors erupted in applause. "More, more!" they shouted. The kids sang several more tunes, then Clay said, "Now it is time for other artists to sing."

Ol' "Doc," Bonnie Blue and Georgie sang an old mountain song from years past. It sounded like they were singing through their noses in a very high pitch. The crowd loved it and gave them tremendous applause. Bonnie Blue looked at the crowd out of one eye and then the other, and turned red as a beet. She had never sung in front of an audience before.

Then Ol' Larry Tuffy brought his hand saw to the porch stage. He had a fiddle bow that he pulled back and forth across the saw as he held the handle between his legs and bent the saw to make different notes. It amazed everyone and they jumped up and down with excitement.

When the party wound down, someone shouted, "Let's do this EVERY summer!" "YES" someone else yelled back, and soon everyone else applauded and whooped in agreement. One by one, everyone thanked the McDougal family for a lovely evening and headed back to their cabin homes.

Exhausted, Mama, Pa, Aunt Olive and the three kids sat on the porch and agreed that it had been a great success.

They went to bed and fell fast asleep. The panther screamed but that night no one on the ridge heard it.

The next morning, Sally Jane came down with paper and pencil and they talked about making a list for next summer's adventures. Luke and Clay started quickly blurting out their own ideas, until Sally Jane said, "Please slow down so I can get them all on paper!" As the discussion proceeded, Sally Jane wrote:

Summer Adventures for Sally Jane, Luke and Clay

"Summer number two"

A. All three kids sleep overnight in the cave

B. Build two tree houses up in the woods and connect with a rope bridge.

C. Ride bikes to town library each week to check out books

D. Make enough money to buy crystal radio kits for all three of us.

E. Listen and learn words of country songs on crystal radio

F. Practice singing to have a trio.

G. Go to new radio station in town and talk to the man who plays the records and get him to like us.

Then, talk the radio man into letting the trio sing on his radio station.

And more things we cannot think of.......

"We will think of some more new plans for making money," said Luke.

There will be lots of new things to do," said Clay. "I hear that a number of people have been seeing black bears coming lower down the mountain. I hope we can see one ourselves."

Luke's eyes almost popped! First panthers, razorbacks, black bears and now a singing trio on the radio! "Wow!" he said, "We do live an adventure every day, don't we?"

The morning of the first day of school arrived. The old yellow school bus came grinding up Panther Creek Road. Sally Jane, Luke and Clay climbed the steps, and Clay made sure that he sat next to Sally Jane.

The three of them sat thinking about what a wonderful summer it had been as the old bus's brakes screeched and it started down the steep slope to the valley.

Clay thought, "What a good friend Sally Jane has been. Luke and I are so lucky to have such a great playmate as our cousin. I can't wait for next summer so we can do all the new things we have on our list."

ABOUT THE AUTHOR

Clyde McCulley was born in Benton, Arkansas, in 1941, the last of six kids born to a sixty-year-old father and a forty-year-old mother. Together, the family tried to eke out a living on a five-acre farm with no running water and a two-holer outhouse.

Clyde was determined to go to college and pursue fine art, ultimately leading him to complete both an MFA and a doctorate in Higher Education Administration.

His memoirs, *The Boy on Shady Grove Road,* brings memories to its readers reminiscent of Mark Twain's *Tom Sawyer and Huckleberry Finn.*

Panther Creek Mountain–The Big Adventure is the first book of stories in a series based on the author's memories and musings of his younger years in Arkansas and mountains of eastern Tennessee.

After a lifetime working as an art instructor and art school administrator, Clyde lives with his wife, Susan, and their cat, Shadow, in Portland, Maine. Clyde's other books, available on Amazon.com, are:

The Boy on Shady Grove Road, a memoir

Journals with prompts for beginning writers:

    Childhood Memories Journal
    I Fondly Remember My Grandparents Journal
    Six Word Stories Journal

Please check out Clyde's websites:
www.mamaswhitegravy.com
www.storynightpress.com
www.ilovejournaling.com